THE SURGEON'S CONVENIENT HUSBAND

AMY RUTTAN

MILLS & BOON

First published in Great Britain 2019
by Mills & Boon, an imprint of HarperCollins*Publishers*
1 London Bridge Street, London, SE1 9GF

Large Print edition 2019

© 2019 Amy Ruttan

ISBN: 978-0-263-07857-2

MIX
Paper from
responsible sources
FSC **FSC™ C007454**

This book is produced from independently certified
FSC™ paper to ensure responsible forest management. For
more information visit www.harpercollins.co.uk/green.

Printed and bound in Great Britain
by CPI Group (UK) Ltd, Croydon, CR0 4YY

Born and raised just outside Toronto, Ontario, **Amy Ruttan** fled the big city to settle down with the country boy of her dreams. After the birth of her second child Amy was lucky enough to realise her lifelong dream of becoming a romance author. When she's not furiously typing away at her computer she's mum to three wonderful children, who use her as a personal taxi and chef.

Also by Amy Ruttan

Unwrapped by the Duke
Alejandro's Sexy Secret
His Pregnant Royal Bride
Convenient Marriage, Surprise Twins
Navy Doc on Her Christmas List
The Surgeon King's Secret Baby
A Mummy for His Daughter
A Date with Dr Moustakas
NY Doc Under the Northern Lights
Carrying the Surgeon's Baby

Discover more at millsandboon.co.uk.

For my mom.
My heart will never be the same.
I love you.

CHAPTER ONE

Anchorage, Alaska

SLEEP. *I NEED SLEEP.*

Ruby was exhausted. She'd just flown to a bush camp at the DEW Line and then back again because of an injured tourist who had been mauled by a bear. They had managed to get the tourist out of the bush camp and to Wainwright, but there had been no surgeon there at the time.

So Ruby had done the surgery. She had stabilized the man and then, with a couple members of her team, she'd brought him back down after the surgery. The Air Ambulance wouldn't have been able to handle it. The man had needed surgery before he could travel. He would have died on the trip in the Medevac.

This was why Ruby loved her job so much.

This is what she lived for. Saving lives on the frontier.

Still, she was beat tired, and very thankful for the midnight sun of the summer. Her internal clock was a bit off, and all she wanted to do now was go home and have a rest. She thought it was morning, but she couldn't be quite certain. And she was pretty sure there was something that she was supposed to do today.

Only she couldn't remember what.

"Dr. Cloutier. I was just looking for you!"

Ruby groaned inwardly and turned around to see Jessica Atkinson, the hospital director at Seward Memorial, and her voice screeching through the fog of her exhaustion reminded her of what she'd forgotten.

Oh. Right.

It was not that she didn't like her, but she was just so exhausted, and she'd completely forgotten about today. Today was the day her husband Aran, Jessica's son, was coming to Anchorage after his honorable discharge.

How could I forget?

She hated herself for forgetting that piece of information. So she plastered on the best, most energetic smile that she could.

She and Aran had been residents together, and when Ruby had had to return to Canada, which had meant giving up all her plans to implement a wilderness trauma team based out of Anchorage, it had been a huge blow. That was when Aran had suggested they get married—so she could stay and finish her work while he enlisted in the Army.

At first Ruby had been against a fake marriage. She hadn't wanted to endanger her plans or Aran's career, but Aran had insisted.

So five years ago they'd got married, and a month ago she'd received word that he'd been injured while on a tour of duty and, after a period of recovery in Germany, would be honorably discharged to his home in San Diego.

She hadn't gone down there because she'd been so busy with her rounds here up north, and she regretted not going. And, judging by the stern look on Jessica's face now, she should *really* be regretting her choice. It had been five years since she'd seen Aran. He'd been her friend, or the closest thing she'd had to a friend, and he'd done her a huge favor.

"Jessica, I haven't seen you in a while. How was your trip to San Diego?" Ruby avoided asking about Aran. She was worried that he was more injured than the initial reports had let on.

"Good, but hot. I much prefer the north." Jessica hesitated, then said, "I'm hoping you can come to my office. I have to talk to you about something."

A shudder ran down Ruby's spine when she saw how uneasy Jessica was. It must be something bad that Jessica wanted to tell her. She had always been pretty good at reading people—it helped when she was dealing with patients, because not everyone told the truth, and helped especially when she was having to deal with people who lived in the bush and didn't have much trust for people who lived in the city.

Or tourists who got drunk and baited a bear.

And, even though Ruby wanted to tell Jessica no, she couldn't. Ruby still felt so guilty about not going down to San Diego to see Aran, even though Aran had sent her an email and told her it was okay that she didn't come. That he didn't mind and knew her work was important.

She should have ignored that and gone anyway.

"Sure." Ruby stifled a yawn and fell into step beside Jessica.

"I know you're tired, Ruby," Jessica said sympathetically. "I heard that you just got back from Wainwright and brought in a bear attack patient?"

Ruby nodded. "A drunk tourist who thought it would be great to get a close-up selfie with a bear, and a bear who thought, *Oh, here's an easy meal.*"

Jessica shook her head and then opened the door to her office. "When will people learn?"

"Never!" Ruby said as she followed Jessica into her office.

"Have a seat."

Jessica walked around and sat down on the

opposite side of the desk and Ruby's stomach twisted into a knot. The last time she had been in this situation she had learned that her work visa was ending and that she was going to be sent back to Canada.

As much as she loved her home in the Northwest Territories, the government there didn't have the money or the manpower to fund Ruby's big aspirations to bring more medical care to the north. Her hope was to one day go back and have the territorial and federal government see what she had done in Alaska. She was getting closer now, but five years ago she hadn't been ready.

Ruby was having an extreme sense of déjà-vu and she didn't like it too much. "Jessica, you're making me a little nervous," she admitted.

"It's nothing bad. Well, *I* don't think it's bad…" Jessica trailed off.

"But I'll think it's bad?"

"You might not be happy about it. I know how particular you are about your team."

That wasn't a good start.

Ruby *was* particular about her team. Working in extreme weather under difficult circumstances and in difficult terrain took a very special kind of person and Ruby was picky about that.

She stiffened her spine and crossed her arms, bracing herself for the worst. "Okay..."

"As you must know, Aran has been honorably discharged from the Armed Forces after he suffered a leg injury."

It was a dig at her and Ruby knew that. She deserved it. "Yes. I do know."

"Aran is your *husband*," Jessica reminded her gently.

"I know, Jessica, and I'm sorry I didn't go down to see him. My work... I had a lot of rounds to finish and..."

Jessica raised her hand. "I get it. I respect it. And Aran understands too. It's just...this whole fake marriage thing..."

"Has Aran found someone else?"

Ruby knew it was possible. Aran was handsome and charming. If she was a different person she might have fallen for him. Every time he walked into a room she could see the dreamy expressions cross women's faces.

She was pretty sure she'd had the same wide-eyed look a few times when she'd used to see him, but she'd kept him at a distance. They'd been work friends—nothing more.

And, since she'd been the only female resident he hadn't slept with during their residency, she had often been paired up with him.

She'd thought his proposal for a fake marriage before he'd left a bad idea, but he'd convinced her it would be fine…

"You're insane." Ruby shook her head and tried to walk away from him.

Aran jogged up beside her and flashed her that bright smile that always melted so many hearts. Including hers, sometimes, but she'd never let him know that.

"So you've told me before," he said. "I'm not wrong about this, though."

Ruby stopped and crossed her arms. "A marriage of convenience? That's something that's only done in the movies or romantic fiction. In real life it's fraud!"

"It's not fraud."

Aran took her hands in his and she tried to control the tremble of excitement he caused in her by his touch.

"We're friends."

"Work friends."

He sighed. "We like each other, at least."

"I'll give you that." She smiled. "What do you get out of doing me this huge favor right before you ship out?"

"I'm doing this for you. I believe in you and you'll owe me one."

"Okay. As long as you're sure."

"Positive. Will you marry me, Ruby Cloutier?"

Ruby shook the thoughts away. She had been attracted to him, but she didn't want any kind of relationship. Her "marriage" to Aran had stopped a lot of friends from trying to set her up. Which had been great. Still, if Aran found someone else she couldn't blame him. She couldn't give him what he wanted.

Can't you?

"Does he want a divorce? If that's what this

is about it's no problem. Honestly, I've thought about getting it done and over with, but I've been so busy…"

Jessica shook her head "It's not that—and anyway you still don't have a Green Card. Immigration will want to interview the both of you now that Aran has been honorably discharged."

"Then what is this about?" Ruby asked, hoping she didn't come off sounding too testy. But she was exhausted and just wanted to get to the point.

"Aran is coming here to work and I want him on *your* trauma team."

Ruby blinked a couple of times. She wasn't certain that she heard Jessica clearly. "What?"

"He has military training and he's a perfect fit."

Only he wasn't. Aran was a fine surgeon, and military training *was* an asset, but she remembered how much he hated the north. How he'd complained bitterly during the winter and through the darkness. He wasn't suited to living up here. He'd told her so enough times.

Maybe he's changed.

Ruby bit her lip. "I vet my team very closely. We all have to work together seamlessly. Aran didn't seem interested in what my team does when I first talked about it. He supported it, yes, but didn't ever seem keen on being a part of it."

It was a nice way of saying she'd thought Aran wouldn't be able to hack it.

Jessica folded her hands across the desk. "It's the only way I can get him to come home. He will be on your team. You have a spot…"

"No offense, Jessica, but I was going to interview someone else for that position."

"Ruby, you can do this favor for me. I've been able to facilitate your stay in this country, and I'm the one who fights with the rest of the board about keeping your vital services. Like you, I think it's important that your venture expands and that you're able to teach your services across the north. Too many people die needlessly because there is no access to healthcare or mental healthcare."

Ruby's mind drifted for a second. Jessica

was right. Too many people died because they couldn't get help right away. Just like her father. Her father who had taught her everything about the north...

"Momma, what's wrong?" Ruby asked, peering through the doorway from the kitchen to the front hall.

She could see her mother leaning against the door, her hand covering her face, her shoulders shaking. Beyond her stood two RCMP officers, their faces crestfallen.

"Momma?" Ruby asked again.

Lieutenant Alexander looked at her. He was her older brother's best friend and his eyes were full of tears. He would tell her the truth. Ruby was a big girl of twelve.

"Ruby, it's your papa. There was an accident at the mine..."

Ruby took a deep breath and tried to shake the memory away.

This was why she was doing what she was doing, but she was selective about who was on her team and who wasn't. Part of her didn't want to take on Aran because she knew how he hated the north, but another part of her realized he was a man with military training.

Although the leg injury worried her...

Sometimes her work took them out into the wilderness, and they had to hike from where they could land the plane. And then there were natural disasters. If he couldn't keep up, then what would happen?

"Okay," Ruby said cautiously. "But he knows that this is *my* team, right? He knows that I'm in charge? The Aran I remember from our resident days was very headstrong."

Jessica nodded and smiled. Ruby could see the relief on her face.

"Yes, he knows that."

"When does he arrive?"

"He'll be here in five minutes. I know you're tired..."

"It's fine," Ruby said, though really it wasn't. She needed to sleep. She'd been up too long, But she had to stay and talk to her husband of five years.

That thought made her chuckle to herself.

She was *really* tired.

There was a knock, and then the door opened and Ruby turned in her chair, expecting to see the same man from all those years ago.

Instead it was a very different man from the one she'd last seen five years ago who walked through the door.

It was shocking what war could do to change a person. The jovial, confident and arrogant man she had known was gone.

Aran was thinner, and instead of the short, buzzed and clean military hair he'd had on their wedding day his dark brown hair was longer, and there were a few grays mixed in there. A scar ran down the side of his face— faint, but still somewhat fresh. The cleft in his chin was hidden by a short-cropped beard and his bearing was not so ramrod-straight as it had once been. He seemed to bear his weight on his left and favored the right leg.

It threw off warning bells. If he couldn't physically handle working on her team he'd be useless to her. Still, Aran was handsome as ever—like on the first day she'd met him. In spite of herself, her heart skipped a beat…

"Dr. Cloutier, you will work with Dr. Atkinson on post-operatives."

Ruby groaned and looked through the throng of residents. Figured that she would get the new guy. The son of the president of the board of directors. She'd heard he was cocky and privileged.

And then she saw him.

He was the most handsome man she'd ever seen. And when those blue eyes settled on her, her pulse kicked up a notch. She had to control herself. She wasn't going to fall for his charms.

"Hi, Dr. Cloutier. I'm Dr. Atkinson." He held out his hand.

She crossed her arms and looked him up and down, but she said nothing. Just grabbed the charts she'd been assigned and walked past him. She didn't have time for any of the kind of games he had to play.

"Okay, then. You're a bit of a hard nut to crack," he said, keeping up with her pace.

She rolled her eyes and handed him a pile of charts. "Here are your cases."

"Thanks," he muttered, and then stood in front of her. "Look, I think the key to a good medical partnership is to at least be friends. We can be civil to each other, can't we?"

Ruby felt guilty for being so cold to him. She was so used to pushing people away. "I suppose... I'm sorry."

He smiled brightly at her. "There—that's better."

She narrowed her eyes and shook her head. "Just do your job and do it well, then we won't have a problem."

"Aran, glad you could finally make it."

Jessica got up and went to embrace her son. He hugged her back, but Ruby could tell that it was grudgingly. In fact, it looked as if her touch caused him pain.

Jessica moved away. "Have a seat, Aran. I was just talking to Ruby about you joining her trauma team."

Ruby watched as he limped to the chair beside her and took a seat. He winced slightly as he sat, but didn't look at her. He was obviously annoyed she hadn't gone down to San Diego, despite what he'd told her. Still, it was the discomfort he was in that worried her. Military man or not, if he was this stiff, in this much pain, he couldn't be on her trauma team. He wouldn't be able to keep up.

"I'm sorry, Jessica," Ruby said.

"For what?" Jessica asked, surprised.

"Aran, you're an excellent surgeon, and your military training would be an asset, but clearly you're not healed enough to be on my team."

She glanced over at Aran and saw he was finally looking at her. His expression was that of a broken man who had seen too much violence. She felt bad, she truly did, but he *had* to be able to handle tough situations. Extreme weather…rough conditions… And she wasn't certain that he could. She hated hurting him like this, but he just wouldn't be able to handle it.

"I can move fine, Ruby. I was just on a very long flight from San Diego to Juneau, then a flight to Anchorage and a cab ride here. Once

I start moving I'll be able to perform my duties adequately," Aran said stiffly.

"Ruby, the board of directors wants Aran on your team. It would be in your best interests—"

"I'm sorry, Jessica." Ruby stood up. "He needs to be in better physical condition. I'm sorry."

Ruby couldn't look at Aran as she left the office. And she didn't get very far before she felt a hand slip around her arm and turn her around. It was Aran and she was surprised.

"Is this fast enough for you?" he asked.

She could see the anger in his eyes. She shook out of his grasp. "So I misjudged your physical endurance…"

"Yes, I'm stiff. Yes, I'm still recovering from my injury. But I can keep up with the work on the trauma team. I can help your team if you just give me a chance." He scrubbed his hand over his face and his expression softened. "Besides, you owe me this. You owe me a favor, remember?"

* * *

Aran held his breath as he looked down into the dark black eyes of his wife and now potentially his boss. When he'd been injured and honorably discharged, he'd been surprised when his mother had showed up in San Diego. She'd never left Alaska—not even when her marriage to his father had been at stake. His mother loved the north.

He'd been glad she'd come, but he'd been disappointed that Ruby hadn't shown. Even though he'd told her she didn't need to come, he'd thought they were friends as well as fake spouses.

He'd always cared for Ruby. Always had a soft spot for her, always desired her. But she'd never been interested. So he'd befriended her. The only woman he'd ever befriended who hadn't turned into a short-lived romance.

Ruby was different from other women he knew. She always had a wall up. So when she hadn't shown up he'd hidden his disappointment. Ruby reminded him of his mother. Always bound to the north and her work. That kind of woman was a kind that he didn't want to get attached to. Yet, he had married Ruby anyway.

He was crazy.

So he hadn't expected his mother to come down to San Diego. And he definitely hadn't expected his mother to offer him a job.

When his mother had offered him a chance to work on an elite trauma team—like working on the front line, but without enemy fire—he'd felt a faint glimmer of hope again. It had crushed him completely when he'd been injured and unable to go back to the front line, and working in a military hospital was something he didn't want to do. He liked to be out in the field, saving lives.

Of course when he'd heard that the leader of this team of trauma surgeons, paramedics and nurses was none other than his fake wife, he'd almost thought about backing down. He knew Ruby wouldn't like it.

He didn't know much about her, because she never let anyone in, but he admired her tenacity—which was why he'd proposed to her. He'd wanted her to make her dream become a reality and he'd valued their work friendship.

It hadn't hurt, either, that Aran had always thought she was one of the most beautiful women he had ever laid eyes on, and for one brief moment in that time just after they were married—just before he shipped out—he'd wished that he could get to know her better. Wished he had more time to bring down those walls of hers.

He had been hoping that their years apart would have changed the attraction he felt for her. Only they hadn't. She was just as beautiful and feisty as ever. With those dark eyes that seemed to pierce right through his soul, her pink full lips, and the black hair that was really a rich dark brown and shot through with hues of auburn.

But she was unobtainable to him, and he knew that a relationship with a woman so connected to her work and to the north would never work out for him.

Now he was really wishing he had said no

to the offer of working up here in Anchorage. He should head back to San Diego.

You made your bed. Now lie in it.

Ruby shook out of his grasp. "Fine. I will give you a chance. But if you can't keep up then I'm sorry but I can't use you on my team."

Aran nodded. "Fair enough."

"Are you going to keep up with physiotherapy?" she asked.

"Yes. I'm about to head there now, and then on to Human Resources."

"I'll walk with you and explain a bit about what I'm doing."

He nodded. "Okay."

Ruby walked slowly. He appreciated that she was trying to be nice, but it was actually harder on his leg than walking quickly.

"We *can* speed it up, you know."

"What?" she asked.

"It's actually better for stretching out the muscles if we move a bit faster."

"Sorry." A blush tinged her warm tawny-colored cheeks.

"It's okay. I've been adamant about getting back into fighting form. I didn't want to lounge away in a hospital bed for long."

She nodded. "Do you mind if I ask exactly how it happened? I was told it was an IED, but nothing else. They didn't give me any more details."

Yes, I do mind.

Only he didn't say that out loud. He hated talking about it—but he didn't have to talk about everything that had happened the night he was injured. He just had to talk about his leg wound. She didn't need to know the rest and he wouldn't tell her. That was *his* business and he wasn't going to let it interfere with his work here. He was going to make damn sure of that.

"No, I don't mind. I was transporting some wounded soldiers to a field hospital and there was an IED explosion."

Cold sweat broke across his brow and he hoped she wouldn't notice. He had thought he was over the initial trauma of talking about it, after he'd recounted what had happened countless times to his superiors and his counsellors during his recovery, but telling Ruby changed the game, and he wasn't sure how he felt about it.

He hoped that she wouldn't pry further. He really didn't want to talk about it, and just thinking about the incident was making him a bit dizzy.

"I'm sorry," Ruby said, and didn't ask anything further. "Well, keep up with the physiotherapy."

Aran nodded curtly. "I will."

"I don't know what your mother has told you about the team I've put together..." She trailed off.

"I remember your ideas for it from back when you were first talking about it."

The blush crept into her cheeks again. "You do?" she asked in amazement.

"I thought it was a good idea—which is why I offered to marry you so you could stay here. I still think it's a good idea. You've done a great job."

"Thanks," she said.

He nodded curtly and looked away. He

couldn't let himself get sucked into her life. She was off-limits. Every relationship was off-limits. He didn't have it in him to pursue one. Not until he got his life back on track.

"Look, I know that it's physically taxing. You've said as much. But I won't hold you back. I have a lot of expertise working in some of the roughest conditions and working with minimal resources to save lives. I would like to continue that work. It's my passion."

A smile tugged on the corner of her lips and made his pulse race. He liked it when she smiled. Since he'd met her all those years ago he hadn't seen her smile genuinely once. Her smiles on their wedding day had been forced and for show.

This smile—it was genuine. It was as if she understood him.

"It's mine as well." She cleared her throat and looked away, the smile disappearing. She stopped, pointing at a door that led to another hall. "Physiotherapy is down the hall. Third door on the left."

Aran nodded. "Thank you."

"Sure." She turned to leave.

"Ruby, maybe…" He couldn't believe what he was about to say. "Can I take you to dinner tonight?"

CHAPTER TWO

"WHAT?" RUBY COULDN'T believe what she was hearing.

"I asked if I could take you, my wife, out to dinner?" His blue eyes were twinkling and he was smiling at her.

"Dinner?" she asked, a bit dumbfounded.

"You know—where people share a meal? We *have* had dinner together before, if you recall."

"I hardly call a sandwich in the cafeteria after doing a round when we were residents a *meal*."

"Well, then, it's time to rectify that, don't you think?"

"Do you think that's wise?" she asked, stunned.

"You *are* my wife," he teased.

She took a step closer and lowered her voice.

"In name only. We're friends, but...really that's all."

"Yeah, but you haven't gained your citizenship yet, have you? Also, since you haven't mentioned divorce..."

Ruby bit her lip. He was right. She had been granted a temporary stay in the country while Aran served, but soon they would have to be interviewed about their marriage before she could obtain citizenship. And then they would have to wait some more time before she could divorce him without it looking suspicious.

Once she got her citizenship she could go back to Canada and visit her relatives.

Do you really want to?

She tried not to think about going back. When she went back to her community it was great to see her mother and her brothers, but it always reminded her of her father's death. How they hadn't been able to get him the help he needed in time. He had died of such a simple thing. If he had been in a city, or had had quick access to a hospital, he would have lived.

She missed her home. She missed the summers spent on the McKenzie, or boating and swimming on Great Slave Lake. She missed flying her brother up to Great Bear Lake to fish and watching muskox across the tundra.

But Ruby didn't want to go back until she was able to fulfill her dream. Completely. Everyone in the north—Alaska, Yukon, Northwest Territories and Nunavut—needed resources. More lives could be saved. And in order to do that she needed dual citizenship.

Aran had done her a huge favor. The least she could do was have dinner with him, she decided.

Big mistake.

All those old feelings she'd had for him—the ones that she'd thought locked away—came rushing back. He was still as charming as ever. Which was why he had been somewhat of a playboy when they were residents. She hadn't been immune to him. She'd just kept him at a distance to protect herself.

Having dinner with him now wasn't exactly keeping her distance from him, but… "Okay.

Sure. I suppose we could," she agreed grudgingly.

"Great. I'll see you about six?"

She nodded. "I'll meet you at the front entrance. Right now I have to check on a patient, and then I'm headed home to sleep."

Aran nodded and then opened the door, disappearing down the hall toward Physiotherapy. Ruby breathed a sigh of relief and rubbed her temples, trying to will the stress headache that was building up to dissipate.

She didn't like to date.

She didn't want to settle down with anyone.

In her job, her life was on the line. She was put in perilous situations. That was no way to raise a family.

Aran was making her question her plans in a way she didn't like. She had been attracted to him once but she'd hoped over their years apart those feelings would change.

They hadn't.

And going out to dinner with him would probably be a big mistake.

She was *not* looking forward to it.

Not even a little?

There was a part of her, deep down, that was. Her job was the most important thing but, whether she liked to admit it or not, she was lonely. It was just a dinner out. What harm could that do?

Ruby looked at her watch. It was a quarter past six and still there was no sign of Aran. It was frustrating. She liked to be punctual. She liked things done a certain way. Aran was late.

So that hadn't changed. Aran had always used to run late for rounds.

She glanced at her watch again.

"A watched pot never boils." That was what her grandmother always said. Her grandmother also always said that Ruby was in a rush to do everything all at once and do it right away. Maybe she was right, but Ruby had learned that you didn't get very far in life just by sitting around or running late.

It was a bad habit of hers to watch the clock,

but watching the clock was important when it came to surgery and saving lives.

A minute could mean life or death. It had been a matter of minutes that had cost her father his life. The delay of the Air Ambulance by that one minute had meant her father didn't have a chance, so Ruby was slightly obsessed with timing.

It didn't do her any good when she was waiting for other people, though. Like now, waiting on Aran to arrive…

"Sorry I'm late," Aran said from behind her, causing her to jump because she hadn't been expecting him to sneak up behind her. He cocked an eyebrow. "You're a bit jumpy?"

"I didn't see you coming." She took a deep breath and tried to calm her racing heart. "Where did you come from, anyways?"

"My cab was late. I had to go back to my hotel room and change."

"Your hotel room? Aren't you staying with your mother?"

"No," Aran said quickly. "I've learned that

my mother and me should *not* live together. I haven't lived with her since I was about eight."

"You had your own place at eight years old?" Ruby teased.

"No." He chuckled. "My parents divorced and I lived with my father. My mother would come down to see me, and when I came up to Anchorage to see her my dad would usually stay in town so that I could stay with him."

"Wow!"

Ruby knew Jessica was divorced, but she'd assumed Aran had stayed with her. And then she remembered Aran had told her he was from San Diego when he was doing his residency, and said how much he loved Southern California.

They'd been friendly with each other, but she was realizing now she really didn't know much about him—and that worried her.

Why had she ever agreed to this sham of a marriage? She shouldn't have, but Aran had been so persuasive. So insistent.

"You okay?" Aran asked.

"Why?"

"You seem a bit tense."

"I'm fine. Sorry, I forgot you said you were from San Diego. I forgot you didn't grow up here."

And it was mistakes like this that made her worry about what they'd done.

"Don't get me wrong—I love my mom. It's just she does certain things a certain way."

"Oh... That's not going to bode well for us, then," Ruby teased.

Aran cocked an eyebrow. "Why's that?"

"I am a bit of a stickler when it comes to doing things a certain way—like being on time." She pointed to her watch and hoped he'd get her joke. She was relieved when he smiled.

"I think it'll be fine." He shoved his hands in his jean pockets. "Where do you want to go?"

"There's a little crab shack down by the water. Do you like crab?"

He nodded. "I do—and it's been some time since I had Alaskan crab."

"Good. I can drive—or we can walk? It's not far from here."

"A walk would be nice. Lead on, Macduff."

She hadn't heard anyone say that to her in a long time. Her father had used to say it all the time, and it brought a memory flooding back to her.

"And where did you see this footprint, Ruby?"

"In the woods. Just before the ice road."

"The ice road is closed and that's all muskeg."

"I know, Papa. I didn't go traveling through that. I was on my way back from the corner store and I saw the footprint. I want to show you."

Her papa smiled. "Okay, show me. Lead on, Macduff."

They walked the way she had taken back from the corner store. She always listened to her parents and kept to the paths she'd been taught to. She knew not to wander in the woods because of bears and other wild animals—not that many would be out in the middle of the day in the summer. Usually the heat and the bugs drove the animals further into the woods. Animals were most likely to come out during the early morning or when it briefly went to dusk.

It was a short walk along the well-worn path from her parents' place, and they stopped when Ruby found the strange footprints she'd never seen before.

Her father knelt down. "Ah, this is a wolverine."

"A wolverine?"

"Yep—and they're nasty. You did good, showing this footprint to me." Her father stood. "Let's go inform the elders and make sure that the other kids keep away from this area. The wolverine has obviously found a food source and will come back, like a bear. A wolverine would attack a young child if it was hungry enough. Remember that, Ruby. Remember that sometimes in the north it's a battle of survival. Eat or be eaten. But you must also respect the land."

"Right, Papa."

"What?" she asked quizzically now, trying to shake the memory away.

Her father had never learned a lot of stories, except what he had been taught when he had been forced to attend a school far from home. The residential school was something he didn't like to talk much about to her. It had been an awful place where his culture and heritage had been forced out of him. Where his language had been stolen. All he had known was what the priests and nuns had taught him, but her father *had* liked Shakespeare.

"It's 'Lay on, Macduff'," Aran remarked offhandedly as he held open the door for her. "'Lead on' is a popular misquote."

"I know. It's just… I haven't heard someone say that in a long time. The way my father said it." She cleared her throat and tried not to let emotion overtake her. She didn't have time to deal with her grief or her sadness.

Aran didn't say any more as they walked down the street from the hospital to the waterfront.

Because it was summer, it was nice to have sunlight so late. It made for pleasant evenings. And it was nice to have the sun because in the winter the sun wouldn't be around long, and there would be a period of time where it just stayed dark, especially the further north you went.

"How long have you lived in Alaska now?" Aran asked.

"This is my sixth year."

"Right!" He chuckled. "We got married five years ago—right after our residency finished. I'm sorry I forgot."

"Well, now I'm going to have to hold it against you."

"Hold what against me?"

"Forgetting our anniversary," she teased.

He shook his head. "So, where in Canada are you from?"

"Behchokǫ̀"

His eyes widened. "I have *no* idea where that is."

Ruby laughed. "Well, it's just outside of Yellowknife, in the Northwest Territories."

"I *do* know where that is. So you're from the north? That makes a lot of sense of why you love it up here."

She nodded. "I went to university and then medical school in London, Ontario. That was a hard transition. I much prefer the north over the city. Although Anchorage is a city, so it must be the north I love."

She was rambling. She knew that. But she really didn't know what else to say to ease the awkward tension that had fallen between them.

"I prefer the south," he said.

"Then why did you come north?" she asked.

"My mother had an opening for a residency."

"I *know* that. That's how we met."

"Right..."

"I mean now...besides our marriage, I guess."

"It's *because* of our marriage," Aran stated, making her blush.

"Oh?"

"Also it's an opening now I've been discharged from the army."

"And your father? How does *he* feel about you moving near your mother?"

Aran's expression hardened. "My father died just before I was deployed."

"Oh, I'm sorry."

And she truly was. She knew what it was like to lose a parent when you were young. It sucked. And she felt bad that she hadn't known that, since they'd got married right before he'd deployed.

Of course. Now it made sense why he'd been so distant during their wedding…

"Look, if you don't want to go through with this it's okay," Ruby offered. Aran was not his usual jovial self.

"No. It's fine," he said quickly.

But he didn't offer a reason why he was so cold. So preoccupied.

"Is it something I did?"

"No," he said tersely.

Before she could back out the court reporter came out into the hallway. "Dr. Cloutier and Dr. Atkinson?"

Aran took her hand and led her into the judge's chambers.

He looked down at her. "Why are you smiling like that?"

"Like what?" Ruby asked. A smile tugged at the corner of her lips.

"Relax. It's okay."

Only it wasn't okay. He'd married her when he'd been grieving. People made a lot of mistakes when they were grieving. Life was like a blur. And when you lost a parent it was as if a piece of your soul had been gouged out from you and you had to relearn the world without that vital piece there. Even twenty years later she was still mourning the loss of her father. She was still grieving him, even though she kept it to herself.

They didn't say much else as they walked the rest of the way to the crab shack. When they got down to the docks the familiar scent of Old Bay seasoning, melted butter and salt water hit her and her stomach growled in response. It had been a long time since she'd come down here and had some Alaskan King Crab. She'd been so busy at work.

Aran held open the door for her and they took a seat in the screened porch that looked out over the Cook Inlet.

"I don't think I've ever been here in all the times I've visited Anchorage," Aran said, looking around.

"Your mom never brought you here? It's an Anchorage institution, apparently."

"This is not my mom's type of place. Brown paper tablecloths, crab and beer... Yeah, so not her thing."

Ruby laughed. "Well, I'm not having any beer tonight. I have a patient to check on when we're done."

"Right—this is the patient who was brought in this morning from up near Wainwright?"

"Yes..." Ruby sighed looking at the menu.

"What can I get you folks today?" asked a waiter, coming up then and interrupting their discussion of the patient.

Which was fine. Ruby really didn't want to talk about her patient at that moment. She was worried about him. He wasn't doing well.

"I'll have an order of crab legs and an iced tea." She handed the menu to the waiter.

"Same," Aran said and handed his menu back.

"Great! I'll be back with your drinks in a moment."

An awkward tension settled between them. She saw Aran was picking at his napkin. What had happened between the two of them? They'd used to be so comfortable around each other. They'd used to be able to work and converse easily.

Of course that had been when they were just friends and not husband and wife. And, really, they hadn't talked much about anything besides work.

"He's not doing well. My patient," Ruby finally said, breaking the tension.

"Oh...?"

"I think an infection has set in. I started a round of rabies shots, obviously, but..."

"Go on," he urged, interested.

"I'm not going to talk about the nature of a bear attack in a restaurant. It was pretty bad. I'm actually surprised that he made it to Anchorage."

Aran nodded. "Yeah, it's best not to talk too much about that when people are eating."

"He's in the ICU, but I have a feeling I'm going to have to open him up again and see if an abscess has formed."

The waiter appeared again just then, with their drinks, and there was a slightly horrified look on his face at hearing the word "abscess." She tried to stifle a laugh.

"Enjoy," the waiter said quickly, before leaving.

Ruby chuckled and Aran smiled.

"See what I mean?" she said. "That waiter was grossed out."

"He did look a bit green around the gills," Aran said looking over his shoulder. "Remember that time when we had to take those first-year medical students on rounds?"

Ruby groaned. "Oh, don't remind me. That was so awful."

"I dragged one young man into the operating room and there was that infected bowel…"

"No, you really need to stop!" Ruby laughed. "That was awful."

"Well, it helped him decide that surgery was not his cup of tea."

Ruby nodded. "It did—and he looked just as green as that waiter."

Aran nodded. "So, who pilots your plane while you're saving lives?"

"Me. I do."

"You're a pilot?" Aran asked, stunned.

"Yes. You seem surprised."

"I haven't met many women pilots. Logically, I know they exist. I've just never met one."

"Well, I grew up in a community where for a long time the only access in or out during different parts of the year was via plane."

Aran cocked an eyebrow. "What do you mean?"

"Up until 2008 the side of Great Slave Lake I lived on could only be accessed in the summer if you drove your car onto a ferry or in the winter when the river froze and you drove your car across it."

Aran's eyes widened. "You mean people drive across ice?"

"Have you never heard of an ice road? They have them up here in Alaska."

"No. I haven't."

Ruby chuckled. "You really are a southern boy."

"So, now you have a bridge?" he asked.

"Yes, there's a bridge crossing the river now, and those communities aren't landlocked during certain seasons. See, when there was ice breaking up the ferry couldn't run, and of course you couldn't drive across it. And ice road seasons are becoming shorter. Still, there are many other places that rely on bush planes to service their communities. When I was old enough I started to take flying lessons. I wanted to be a pilot. My older brother is a bush pilot."

"Is he a doctor too?"

"No!" Ruby smiled as she thought of the time her older brother had been fishing and got a splinter. He had passed out when she'd had to remove it. "He turns green much like the waiter."

Aran laughed softly. "You're pretty strong-willed. It's one thing I've always liked about you."

"I'll take that as a compliment."

"Do."

His blue eyes twinkled and she could feel warmth flooding her cheeks. She looked away.

"Why don't you tell me about your time in the Army? You never did say much about it the few times you emailed."

His expression hardened and he went back to fiddling with his paper napkin. "We don't need to talk about that."

"I think we do," Ruby said. "I'm very selective about my team. You know that I am. I need to know about your time overseas so that I can ease my anxiety about the nepotism your mother seems to have imposed on me. Also, if the Immigration people come… I mean…we're *married*. We've been married for five years and I should know about what happened to you in those years."

* * *

Ruby had a point, but it didn't mean that Aran liked it. The military had been so important to him. His father had been in the military too, but he had been a doctor who worked on base and never served time overseas, like Aran had. It was another reason why his parents had split.

His dad had loved the military life and his mother had not. She'd loved Anchorage. She'd loved the hospital that she'd helped build from the ground up and she wouldn't leave Alaska for anything. Not even for her child.

Aran understood her love for her career now. Especially since he'd been mustered into the Armed Forces and become a military surgeon. He'd loved serving his country. It had been the most important thing to him.

But now it was gone.

He couldn't serve.

So, no, he really *didn't* want to talk about it—but Ruby was right. They could get into a lot of trouble for what they'd done. A marriage of convenience so that Ruby could stay in the country and work…so that his mother wouldn't lose Ruby's contribution to what she'd sacrificed everything for. And that was Seward Memorial.

Aran had done it for Ruby, though. He'd agreed to the marriage because of Ruby and her passion for her work.

"I really can't talk about where I was. It was a war zone. It is still a war zone."

Ruby nodded, but persisted. "Tell me more about the IED blast?"

Sweat broke across his brow and he took a sip of his iced tea. He tried to stop the thundering in his ears as his pulse quickened. He closed his eyes and tried to drown out the sounds of the blast.

Pain.

Aran woke up lying in sand. He couldn't move his leg. He cursed and tried to orient himself to his surroundings. The sun was bright against the sand and the air was filled with smoke and gasoline.

Oh, God.

He looked around to try and find mem-

bers of his unit, but all he could see was the truck on its side, on fire, and bodies scattered around the dunes.

"Yuck!"

Aran's eyes snapped open and he saw a look of horror on Ruby's face. "What's wrong?"

"Pass the sugar."

Aran slid the sugar shaker toward her and Ruby dumped some sugar in her iced tea.

He couldn't help but chuckle.

"You have to ask for sweet tea," he gently reminded her.

"I know and I always forget. In Canada, iced tea *is* sweet tea." Ruby stirred her drink and took a sip. "Better."

The waiter returned then, with their food, and he was eyeing Ruby with interest and fear. "Is everything okay, miss?"

"Fine," Aran said. "She just wanted sweet tea. Canadians—what can you do?"

Ruby's eyes narrowed and Aran tried not to laugh. He couldn't remember the last time he'd really laughed and enjoyed himself. There had never been much time when he was at the front. There had been too many broken soldiers to mend. Wounded civilians too. It had all been just a big mess.

The waiter left.

"I don't think he's coming back to this table in a hurry," Ruby teased as she cracked open a crab leg.

"I agree. We've scared him off."

Ruby nodded.

"Do you know when Immigration will be wanting to interview us?" Aran asked in a hushed tone.

"No. I assume, though, now that you're back in Alaska and honorably discharged, it will be sooner rather than later."

Aran nodded. "I'm willing to make this work you know."

"Our marriage?" she asked.

"Right. So that you can get your citizenship, I mean. I still believe in your work like I did five years ago."

She blushed again. "Thank you. I appreciate that. It means a lot to me. I have a lot of big plans, and Seward Memorial is the first step in making them a reality. I really do appreciate the favor. The sacrifice you made."

"Thank you," he said. "And I really do admire the work you've done and the team you've set up."

"You don't need to patronize me," she muttered.

"I'm not. It's true. What you're doing for people who are out there, away from a hospital... It's important. You're out there saving lives."

She nodded, but didn't say anything further, and he couldn't help but wonder what had changed. Had he said something wrong?

Aran thought it best not to press it.

They ate in silence.

When they were finishing up Ruby's pager went off. She wiped her hands and looked at it, frowning when she saw the message.

"Shoot," she mumbled.

"What's wrong?"

"My bear attack patient—he needs surgery. It's just what I thought. I have to get back to the hospital." Ruby motioned to the waiter.

"Can I help you, miss?" the waiter asked.

"The bill, please."

"Separate or...?"

"Together," Aran said.

The waiter nodded and disappeared.

"Aran, you don't..."

"I asked you out to dinner. This is my treat. You go back to the hospital and I'll meet you there. I'd like to help. I'd like to learn how you do things."

Ruby's expression softened. "Thank you— and, yes. Of course. Come to the operating floor and we'll get you scrubbed in."

"Okay. I'll see you there."

Ruby slid out of her chair and moved quickly through the busy restaurant.

It was not a long walk to the hospital, he thought. But his leg was a bit stiff. Yeah, it helped to move it, but he had been doing too much today to be able to show her that he could keep up. So he was going to take a cab back to the hospital.

Hopefully the pain would subside a bit so that he could be in the operating room with her, because that was the last thing he needed anyone to see.

He didn't need anyone to see his pain.

CHAPTER THREE

RUBY WAS HOPING that Aran would show up soon, because in another minute she wouldn't be able to wait any longer and she'd have to go and scrub in. Her patient from Wainwright was in the operating room and being prepped for surgery.

Come on Aran. Don't be late this time.

Ruby tied back her hair and then put on a scrub cap. As she tied it on Aran appeared, in scrubs, and seemed ready to go.

Thank goodness.

"I was just about to scrub in," she said as he moved past her to grab a scrub cap.

"I know. That waiter was slow."

He winced slightly and it made her uneasy.

"Are you okay?" she asked.

"Fine. A little stiff, but I can handle the operating room. It's an infected abscess, yes?"

"As far as I know. My plan is to go in and remove what I can of the infection, then pack him and place a drain. That bear tore open his abdomen and I'm not so sure it was completely clean."

"Jeez…" Aran said. "He's lucky to be alive."

"Yes—and this is why drinking and hunting don't mix."

"I thought most camps up there were dry?" he asked.

"They are. He snuck some beer in. The State Troopers are involved, and there are fish and wildlife troopers dealing with the bear. Unfortunately the bear loses completely, because he'll be destroyed. Once they have the taste for… Well, the bear might come back to the camp and it would pose a threat."

Ruby did feel bad for the bear. It wasn't the bear's fault that it had attacked. The man had been reckless and stupid. He'd done something illegal by bringing alcohol to a dry camp. To survive up in remote locations like that you needed your wits about you.

Eat or be eaten. That was what her father

and her older brother had taught her about surviving in the north. They'd told her to trust her instincts and be wary of strangers as well. Ruby totally relied on her instincts. They'd saved her countless times.

They walked to the scrub room and started scrubbing in.

"Just follow my lead," Ruby said.

"I have put together men who were in worse shape than this patient," Aran stated.

"I'm sure, but this is *my* patient and my operating room." She shook her hands before drying them off with a paper towel. She slipped on a paper mask and headed into the operating room, where a scrub nurse was waiting to help her on with her gown and gloves.

She didn't doubt that Aran had worked on worse cases, but Ruby liked control, and this was her patient and her OR. She was going to do things *her* way.

She took a calming breath. A little moment of meditation before she approached the operating table. She could hear the door behind her open—the door to the scrub room. She knew that Aran was getting into his gown and being gloved.

She wasn't sure how this was going to work out, and she was sort of kicking herself for inviting him into her operating room. She liked to work with surgeons she knew. Surgeons she'd worked with before. Aran might be an excellent surgeon, but he was still an unknown factor in the calm and order that she demanded in her operating room.

This was why she was one of the best trauma surgeons in the north. This was why she led such an elite rescue team. Because things were done her way, in her fashion.

It worked.

It saved lives.

She took her place at the operating table while a resident read off the chart.

"Patient is Albert Weinstein, thirty-three. The surgery is to remove an abscess that has formed on his abdominal wall secondary to an…"

The resident cleared her throat and Ruby

knew she was having a hard time reading it because it was a pretty vicious injury.

"Evisceration," Ruby stated.

The resident nodded. "Evisceration that was repaired by Dr. Cloutier in Wainwright. Patient was deemed stable to travel and be placed in the ICU at Seward Memorial. The patient's white cell count has increased, and he spiked a temperature this afternoon. This led to a CT scan that confirmed an abscess has formed."

"Thank you, Dr. Marks," Ruby said.

Aran stood on the opposite of the table. "Ready, Dr. Cloutier?"

Ruby nodded at him and looked down at her patient. *Foolish man.* Well, whether he was foolish or not, she was going to save his life.

Ruby finished her chart, even though her shoulders were aching. She had managed a small nap when she'd got home, before she went out to dinner with Aran, but her body was telling her that it hadn't been enough.

She rubbed her eyes. She needed to finish

her work here and then find a place to crash. Even though she should go home, she didn't want to leave her patient. She wanted to monitor him closely while he was in the intensive care unit. So she needed to be close by, just in case anything happened to him.

"Hey," Aran said as he approached the charge desk.

"Hey." She nodded, not looking up from her work.

"Your patient's family is here—and his brothers who were up at the hunting camp too. They're looking for an update."

Ruby sighed. This was the part of the job she hated. She hated having to deal with the families of her patients. Good or bad, she just found it difficult.

"Okay." Ruby finished off her chart and set the binder back behind the ICU charge desk. "Where are they?"

"In the waiting room. You want me to come with you?" he asked.

"No, it's fine."

"It doesn't look fine. You look like you'd rather do anything but talk to the family."

"Well, that's the truth. Especially when I don't have any answers."

Only that wasn't completely it. Talking to families was hard when you were a trauma surgeon most times anyway, but it also evoked something in her. Something she didn't like to think about.

She remembered what it had been like, walking down the halls of Stanton Territorial Hospital in Yellowknife so that they could view her father. How the doctor there had tried to offer his condolences to them. But all Ruby had been able to see was her father, lying there under a white sheet. His eyes had been closed and he was gone.

Just gone.

The one person who had always been her rock was no longer there.

It was a pain that haunted her still. And when she had to tell family members that their loved one was really ill and might not make it, or that their loved one had passed away, the pain in their faces brought it all back.

It was the worst part of the job for Ruby. If she didn't have to deal with the families, it would be so much better.

Ruby walked numbly toward the quiet room where her patient's family had been told to wait for her. Her pulse was racing as she saw a little girl, clutching her mother's hand. The little girl looked to be about twelve.

Just like she had been.

Oh, Creator.

"Hey, are you okay?" Aran asked.

Ruby nodded. "Just give me a moment."

"Sure."

She could hear the sympathy in his voice.

"I don't envy you. I never had to do this in the Army. I would patch the soldiers up and get them stable enough to travel to a military hospital. I didn't have to contact significant others or children about their loved ones."

Ruby nodded. "I hate this part."

"What about when your patients live? Surely you don't mind delivering *that* news?"

"I don't like interacting with families at all—but, yeah, when they live and pull through that is so much better." She took a deep breath.

"Do you mind if I come in with you?" Aran asked. "I haven't done this in a while—not since I was a resident, and even then it was in a military hospital. I'd like to see how you handle it."

"Sure. Let's go."

Aran opened the door for her and Ruby walked into the room. The family stood, but their gazes didn't go to her—they focused on Aran.

"How is he, Doctor? How is my husband?" asked the woman holding the little girl's hand.

Aran glanced at Ruby. "You'll have to ask his doctor. This is Dr. Ruby Cloutier—the one who brought him down from Wainwright—and she's his surgeon."

Everyone turned and looked at her.

Her pulse began to race as they looked at her with disbelief. It wasn't the first time someone had looked at her like that and it wouldn't be the last. She was short and she was a woman.

People always assumed it was a man who was the surgeon and not her.

"Yes, I'm Dr. Cloutier, and I did the first surgery on Mr. Weinstein in Wainwright."

"How is he?" his wife asked.

"Stable, but…" Ruby trailed off as she looked down at the little girl staring up at her. It broke her heart. "He's in the intensive care unit. Mrs. Weinstein, I can have a child life specialist paged and then I can talk to you about your husband's condition."

"Mommy…?" the little girl asked.

Mrs. Weinstein nodded. "Yes, that's probably for the best."

Ruby nodded and quickly left the room to page someone to take the child to a play area. It wasn't long before Bonnie, a child life specialist, came down to the quiet room.

Ruby led Bonnie over to the little girl. "This is my friend, Bonnie, and she's going to take you to do some crafts while I talk to your mom, okay?"

The little girl nodded and took Bonnie's hand as she was led from the room.

"How bad is it, Doc? I'm his brother and I remember you from the camp."

Ruby glanced up at the man. "It's bad—and you need to prepare yourself. I'm not going to lie. Your husband's condition is severe, Mrs. Weinstein. I was able to repair the damage to his internal organs and stabilize him before flying to Anchorage, but he's developed an infection and an abscess has formed. Right now he needs to stay in the intensive care unit while the infection drains and while the wound is open and packed."

"Oh, God…" Mrs. Weinstein sat down.

Ruby wanted to chastise her patient's brothers about safety, and drinking while dealing with large predators, but she didn't. She fought the urge.

"We're not from Alaska," Mrs. Weinstein stated. "We're from Kansas. Can we get him transferred there?"

"Eventually," Ruby said. "We can't move him right now. If we do, he will die."

"He can't stay here. He *has* to come home,"

Mr. Weinstein's brother insisted. "When can we move him?"

Only he wasn't looking at her. He was looking at Aran again, which infuriated her.

"He can't be moved," Aran stated. "Did you not clearly hear what Dr. Cloutier said?"

"We'll stay," Mrs. Weinstein said with resignation. "We'll stay until he can be transferred to Kansas."

Ruby nodded. "I'll send in a social worker to help you with arrangements and someone will take you up to see him shortly."

Mrs. Weinstein nodded and Ruby took that moment to leave the room and catch her breath as well as control her anger. This was why she hated dealing with families. They couldn't think rationally.

But there was a side of her that sympathized with them. You didn't think rationally when you were grieving. She got that. She understood that well.

"Dr. Cloutier?"

Ruby turned to see a nurse coming toward her. "Yes, Janet?" she said.

"There's a call for you on line three. It's a man from the United States Citizen and Immigration services."

"Immigration?"

It took a moment to let the word really sink in. Her stomach dropped to the soles of her feet.

"Immigration…" Janet said nervously.

Ruby's stomach sank. "Thank you, Janet."

Janet nodded and headed back to the charge desk.

Ruby groaned as Aran came out of the waiting room. He'd stuck around, waiting for the social worker to arrive.

"What's wrong?" he asked.

"Immigration is calling me."

Aran's brow furrowed. "They want to check up on us, I suppose."

"Yeah…" Ruby sighed nervously and began to wring her hands.

"Well, you should take the call."

Ruby nodded, but she really didn't want to.

They made their way into an empty doctors' lounge and Aran locked the door behind them.

She just stared at the phone flashing, her heart racing as she picked up the line.

"Dr. Cloutier speaking."

"Dr. Cloutier—this is Agent Bolton of the United States Citizen and Immigration Services, about your Green Card application."

"Yes?"

"We've been informed that your husband, Dr. Aran Atkinson, has been honorably discharged from the Armed Forces and has since returned to Anchorage. Is that correct?"

"Yes, he arrived yesterday." She was glad her sleep deprivation hadn't deprived her from remembering that it was early the next morning.

"That's great. We'd like to set up a time to come and meet both of you in the next couple of days—at your convenience. We'd like to do a last interview and some paperwork before we can approve your Green Card and citizenship."

"Sounds great. Why don't you email me a few dates and I'll arrange our schedules?"

"Perfect. We look forward to meeting you both, Dr. Cloutier."

Ruby hung up the phone and felt as if the room was spinning. This was why she should have said no when Aran had suggested marriage to her five years ago.

"Well? Do you know what they want?" Aran asked.

She nodded. "I do. They probably know that you're not living with me. That you've checked into a hotel."

"Right..."

Ruby sighed. "They want to meet with us both—probably at *our* house."

"Did they *say* our house?" Aran asked.

"No. They didn't. But it really doesn't make sense that a husband and wife live apart, now, does it?"

"You're right."

"They want to meet us at our convenience." Ruby bit her lip nervously.

"Okay. So we'll set up a time, right?"

Ruby nodded. "I think we need to do a bit more than that, though."

"Oh?" Aran asked.

She couldn't believe she was about to say this, but to make this work it was the only solution—even if it was a dangerous one.

"I think you need to check out of your hotel and move in with me."

Aran wasn't sure if he was hearing Ruby correctly. Had she actually just suggested that he move in with her? He had planned to get his own place in Anchorage. He didn't have plans to live with *anyone*—not even the woman who was technically his wife.

He was better off alone—especially since the accident. He had really bad bouts of night terrors and he didn't want to scare Ruby or even to have her know. He didn't want anyone to know. The only person it affected was him.

Living with Ruby?

That was *not* a good idea.

He didn't want to get married—ever.

You are *married, remember?*

Well, he didn't want to get emotionally involved with anyone. Not after seeing what had happened to his parents. Not after living through that IED explosion. He didn't have any desire to be with anyone. He was better off alone.

Moving in with Ruby was a bad idea. Why had he offered to marry her in the first place?

You believed in her. You still do.

But he was supposed to be still serving overseas. He wasn't supposed to be here, broken and no longer doing what he loved.

"Aran?" Ruby asked, breaking his chain of thought.

"What?"

"I said I think you should check out of your hotel and move in with me."

"That's what I thought you said." Aran ran his hand through his hair.

"It would look better if we were living together since we've been married these last five years."

She bit her lip, and he could tell that she wasn't exactly thrilled with the prospect.

"It's not permanent. It would just be until everything's cleared up and we can divorce."

Say no. Say no.

Only he couldn't. She was right. The most logical thing to do was move in with her. Even if he thought it was the worst idea ever. He wasn't emotionally in the right place to move in with any one.

Not after what had happened overseas.

Not after his whole unit had been wiped out and he'd been the only one to survive.

Even his survival had been pure dumb luck, and there were days when he wished he *hadn't* survived.

Don't think like that.

Aran closed his eyes and took a few deep, calming breaths as the negative thoughts threatened to take over, as the post-traumatic stress started getting to him.

"Aran? Are you okay?" Ruby asked cautiously.

"Fine." Only he wasn't.

"You're sweating."

"I'm fine," he snapped, and then scrubbed a hand over his face.

"Is it because of my suggestion? I know it's

a big deal—and, trust me, I'm not a fan of it either."

"It's not your fault." Aran sighed. "It was at my suggestion we got married and now we have to live with the consequences. You're right. It makes sense that we move in together."

She nodded. "So is that a yes?"

"Yeah, I'll move in with you."

What had he done?

CHAPTER FOUR

THE NEXT EVENING, after their shifts in the emergency room, was when the big move was going to happen. Not that it was really a big move. Aran didn't have much to pack from his hotel room. The rest of his things, and some of the things he'd been left by his late father, were in storage back in San Diego.

Aran's stepmother had the majority of the stuff, and Aran's half-siblings had all had things left to them, but Aran hadn't wanted to bring the few things he'd been left up to Anchorage, because he wasn't sure how long he would stay here.

So he packed what he had and shoved it into his Army duffel bag.

Ruby was waiting in her car. He'd told her there was no point in her coming in and helping him. He threw his duffel bag into the back of her truck and slowly climbed into the passenger side of the cab.

"You good?" Ruby asked, and her voice rose slightly.

He could tell that she was just as uneasy about this as he was.

"As good as I'll ever be," Aran admitted.

"Okay. Let's go." Ruby pulled the stick and put the truck into gear. He could hear the drive shaft grind and the truck lurch.

"You know how to drive stick?" he asked, amused.

"Yes. That's all I've ever driven. But this truck needs work and I haven't had time to get it to the shop."

"It's an old truck."

Ruby glanced at him briefly. "So?"

"So you're a surgeon—a *well-paid* surgeon..."

"Who has bought her own bush plane... Well, with help from the hospital," Ruby interjected. "The plane and its upkeep is where I spend my free money. I need to have the best plane in order to save lives in the bush."

"Ah..."

Ruby smiled. "I will admit I'm a better pilot than I am a driver."

"Well, I can take a look at your truck when I get a day off, or something."

"You know how to fix trucks?"

Aran shrugged. "My dad and I restored an old Trans Am, and I did some tinkering when I was overseas."

"I would appreciate that."

Then Ruby moaned.

"What's wrong?" Aran asked.

"We were friends for…what?…like, a year before we were both at the end of our residency and yet we know nothing about each other."

"Well, we hung out in a group, and really all we talked about was medicine. You wanted it that way, usually."

"Right…"

He could hear the nervousness in her voice.

"Hey, we haven't set a date for the interview. Let's take this chance to get to know each other beyond the hospital."

Ruby nodded. "Okay. Because I'm worried no one will believe we're married."

"Ditto."

Ruby glanced at him. "What did you tell people about me?"

"What?" he asked. "What do you mean?"

"What did you tell people about your wife—which is me?" she teased.

"I told people that you were a surgeon. A talented surgeon in Anchorage. Sometimes there wasn't a whole lot of time to chat..."

"We're under fire, Captain!" Aran shouted.

"Get the wounded out of here. Pack them and transport them."

Aran nodded and went about packing the wound of the soldier he'd been working on. He taped over the open wound so that nothing would get in there. Or nothing more. Because they were working on these wounded men in a tent, in the middle of the desert.

He shook away that memory.

"So, what did you tell people about *me*?" he asked.

"Most people at the hospital know who you are."

"Yes, but you always made it clear you were only interested in surgery. How did I win you over? Was it my charm? Was it my good looks?"

Ruby chuckled. "Something like that. Yes, I guess you can say people were a little shocked, but since your mother was thrilled about it they really didn't question it. We were always working together and butting heads. I guess a lot of the staff thought it was inevitable."

Inevitable.

Before the war he'd thought that might be true, but right now he wasn't so sure.

It wasn't a long drive from his hotel to her home. She lived just outside of town, down a windy dirt road off Glen Highway Number One, in the middle of a copse of hemlock and black spruce. It was a small log cabin, like something out of the frontier days.

"This is a nice place," he said, and he meant it.

He had always been partial to log homes—

especially log homes that were outside the city. He loved San Diego, and being close to the beach, but he preferred the mountains. He loved spending time up in Yosemite, and had climbed El Capitan twice. Of course that had been when he was younger and his leg hadn't been mangled to heck, with pins holding the remnants together.

"Thanks."

She pulled out her keys and tossed them to him. He caught them easily.

"Just go on in. You can use the guest bedroom on the main floor. I'm going to chop some wood for the night."

"You chop wood too? Are you some kind of lumber jill?"

She picked up the ax and looked confused. "No, but I've been chopping wood since I was able to swing an ax."

"Next you're going to tell me you built this home."

"No. *That* I didn't do. When would I have had the time?"

She winked and he couldn't help but smile.

Aran watched her walk away, admiring the sway of her hips and carrying the large ax as if it weighed nothing. Her black hair was tied back. She was tough. He had to give her that. And her toughness, her indomitable spirit, attracted him.

He admired her. Still. Time hadn't changed that fact.

He unlocked the door to her house and stepped in. The place was sparsely decorated, but it was modern, mixed with the rustic feel of a northern cabin, and most important it was comfortable. It was way better than a hotel room.

He set his stuff down on the bed and then heard a dog barking wildly outside. He moved quickly, his pulse quickening, hoping it wasn't a wolf or a coyote—even if the bark didn't sound particularly vicious.

Aran found the back door that led to where Ruby was chopping wood. He was about to call out to her, but then he saw what was barking and relaxed.

There was a dog house outside. And a long

chain. The barking dog in question was bouncing from the top of his dog house to the ground and happily wagging his tail. It was a beautiful sled dog, with white and black fur. Its eyes were brilliant blue and the tail that was wagging back and forth was quirked up in a question mark.

"You okay?" Aran asked.

The dog's ears perked and its eyes focused on him. It didn't growl, but Aran knew it was on alert.

"Chinook, it's okay. This is Aran. He's a *friend*."

As soon as Ruby said "friend" Chinook came bounding over and sniffed him cautiously—but only for a moment before the question mark tail began to wag.

"You can pet him," Ruby said as she set up another log. "He's friendly and very well trained."

Aran reached out and the dog closed his eyes and leaned into the head scratch. Aran couldn't help but smile. When Chinook had

had enough, he bounded down the back steps and ran around the yard, barking happily.

"When did you get a dog?" he asked.

"About two years ago."

"He's beautiful."

"I know. He's pretty special. He keeps me company."

"I'm glad you're a dog person," he said.

"I never did understand that."

"What?" he asked.

"Dog person or cat person. How could you *not* be a dog person? Dogs are awesome. Cats are cool too. Why does it have to be one or the other?"

"You're right. I don't get it either."

"This is why we're friends."

"I thought we knew nothing about each other?" he teased.

"Right." She continued chopping wood while Chinook trotted back for more petting.

"You're not worried about your dog running out onto the road?" Aran asked.

"No," Ruby said. "He knows his territory. He has a long chain and he protects the property when I'm gone. He prefers the outdoors. Alaskan Malamutes do. I tried keeping him inside and it was a disaster."

She brought the axe down, splitting the wood.

Aran sat on the back steps. "Sure you don't want help with that?"

"No, I'm fine. I can do it on my own."

"You like to be in control, don't you?" he asked.

"Don't you?" she asked, before bringing the ax down again, splitting off another piece.

"I do."

"When you grow up in the north you have to be in control. It's a hard life." Her expression changed and she set up another log.

"How do you mean?" he asked.

"It's cold," she stated.

But he had a feeling that she was hiding something. There had been other times in the past when he got too close to something and she'd thrown up a wall. What was she hiding?

Of course he was hiding things too. He was hiding the horror he'd experienced on the front. Hiding the pain and scarring of his leg. Who was he to judge?

"I know that. Although it's not that cold right now." And then he slapped his arm where a mosquito had landed. "Buggy, but not cold."

A slight smile quirked on Ruby's lips. "It's better when you get closer to the city. A lot of people make their way down to the city. To die."

He was confused by that statement. "What do you mean, people go to the city to die?"

"There's more resources there. When it gets too hard to live on the land they go to the city to die. You have to be healthy to live in the remote areas of northern Alaska and Canada. One small mistake and your life could be over. That's how my father died."

She brought the ax down and Aran noticed she brought it down harder.

So that was it. That was what she was hiding.

"So that's why you're a trauma surgeon?"

She glanced at him. Her dark eyes flashed with anger and annoyance. He'd hit a nerve.

"Don't try and figure me out."

"I can't help it. Patients don't always tell you the whole truth," he said. "It's my job to figure it out."

"Yeah, I guess," she remarked as she set down her ax and collected up the wood she'd cut.

Aran got up and helped her pick up the wood, following her inside, where she set it next to the fireplace. She knelt down and Aran handed her the wood so she could stack it neatly.

"Sorry about your dad," he said.

She shrugged. "It was a long time ago. I don't really want to talk about it."

"Isn't this the kind of stuff that we *should* be talking about?" he asked.

"What do you mean?" Her dark eyes were flashing again in annoyance.

"This Agent Bolton is going to want to ask us in-depth questions about each other. Fine, we live together, but how well do we know each other?"

"Married couples have secrets. They don't always know everything about each other."

She was right about that. He only had to look at his own parents for confirmation of that.

His dad had been up in Alaska on vacation when he'd met his mother, and it had been love at first sight. Although in reality probably more like lust at first sight. They'd married after a week of dating and the next month his mother had discovered she was expecting him.

Aran's father had tried to like Alaska, but he hadn't been able to stand the cold winters, and Aran's mother had been focused on her job with the hospital board of directors and research grants. Aran's father had raised him.

And then they'd got divorced. Aran's mother had tried to take care of him, but Aran had been left alone with nannies and babysitters all the time and he'd hated it. So he'd been sent to San Diego to live with his father.

It had been the best thing for him. He'd had

a good life there. He didn't know his mother that well, and he wasn't close with her, but he'd loved living with his father and then his stepmother.

But Ruby was right. His parents had rushed into marriage and hadn't known anything about each other. They'd acted on impulse and look how that had turned out.

Didn't you act on impulse in agreeing to marry Ruby before you shipped out?

"I think secrets are a dangerous thing," he stated. "I think we should try to get to know one another the best we can."

Ruby didn't look convinced. She finished stacking the wood and stood up. "You hungry?"

"Sure."

"Good. I'll make something."

She went into the kitchen and Aran sighed. He was trying to help her. Why was she being so stubborn? What was she hiding about her father's death?

You're hiding something too.

* * *

Ruby didn't really want to think about her father and how he'd died. That was how she got through the days. She didn't exactly bury the grief that she carried around, but she'd learned to compartmentalize it so that she could continue with her life.

If she didn't do that it would eat away at her. She would break down. And there was no time for that. There was no time for emotions.

Even after all this time the grief was still there. That gnawing pain that ate away at her very soul. It was an ache that she'd got used to. So, no she didn't want to talk about it.

Not with Aran, not with anyone.

That was her pain to bear. It had nothing to do with her Green Card.

It was what had shaped her. What had made her who she was today.

She opened the fridge and frowned when she saw there wasn't much. Actually, there was nothing but some orange juice and an onion.

"What are you going to make with such a variety of ingredients?"

She glanced over her shoulder to see Aran standing there. His eyes were twinkling and she couldn't help but laugh. "I've been busy."

"Does pizza come out this far?" he asked.

"Yes." Ruby picked up her phone. "Any particular kind of pizza?"

"Nope. I'm not picky."

Ruby called the local pizza place and ordered her usual and some drinks, as she didn't think that orange juice and pizza would go together particularly well. "Should be here in about an hour," she said as she set the phone down.

She leaned across the island counter. Aran had taken a seat on one of the barstools on the other side of the island and was facing the bank of floor-to-ceiling windows that faced out back.

Chinook was bouncing back and forth like a lunatic and she couldn't help but laugh at his antics. When she had time off she liked to take him on a hike down to the lake, so that he could go swimming and stretch his legs. In the winter she'd often set up a small sled and run him around.

"Your dog is a bit crazy," Aran said.

"I like a bit crazy."

He grinned at her. "Why doesn't that surprise me?"

"And what's *that* supposed to mean?" she asked, straightening up and crossing her arms.

"You're as bad as those smoke jumpers who fight forest fires."

"Hey, I know a lot of those men and women. In fact one of my nurses is a former fire jumper. He's a valuable asset to my team. One I picked out specially."

"I know—and I'm one you didn't get to pick out."

"Right. I was forced to add you to my team."

He looked at her. "Just like I was forced to ask you to marry me to keep you here."

She pursed her lips together. She couldn't really argue that point. She didn't like it too much, but it was true. He had done her a big favor. She really owed him one but she was completely stressed out by this whole charade.

"I'm thankful for that, you know, but the north is harsh."

"Look, I know you don't think I understand the north, and maybe I don't, but my training speaks for itself. I've worked in harsh conditions and under fire."

She didn't doubt him. During the surgery he'd done well. There'd been a few things he'd did that she hadn't exactly agreed with, but that was a matter of preference. It hadn't endangered the patient. Still, she didn't know him as he was now. She didn't know much about him. They had to change that.

"How do feel about flying?" she asked.

"Like in an airplane?"

"No, in a glider," she retorted.

"Well, if you mean your bush plane, not a jet plane, then I would be fine. I've never been in a bush plane, but I'd be willing to fly in one."

Ruby smiled. "I'm due to make a trip up to Whitehead tomorrow. It's a routine check on a nurse practitioner who's in the village. I'd like you to come."

He nodded. "Sure. I'd like that."

Ruby smiled. "We might have to do some minor surgeries. The nurse practitioner saves up routine operations for when I come. For any big surgeries that need to be done in a hospital she either calls me or the Air Ambulance to fly the patients out."

"Minor? So, like gall bladders or things like that?" he asked.

"Yes. Is that a problem?"

"Nope. It sounds good. I look forward to flying with you."

"Good."

Although she wasn't too sure about this either. She wasn't sure how it was going to go tomorrow, and she wasn't sure how well they were going to work together. But it was better that she tested it out this way instead of being thrust into an emergency situation with him, where everything might potentially fall apart and cost lives.

There was a knock at the door and Chinook went around the front to visit Sam the pizza guy who was very familiar with Chinook and his behavior. Sam was her neighbor, and he often took care of Chinook when Ruby had to fly out to remote locations.

"Hey, Doc," said Sam when she answered the door. "Bigger order. You have company?"

Leave it to Sam, who had been operating his pizza place in the area for a long time, always to poke his nose into everyone's business.

She really didn't want it to become neighborhood gossip that her husband was back, or that she was even married. But then a thought occurred to her that maybe this *would* be a good thing. It would solidify their fake marriage for Agent Bolton when he came to check up on them.

"I do have company, Sam." Ruby stepped back and Aran stood up. "My husband has been serving overseas the last five years and he's finally come home. Sam, I'd like to introduce you to my husband, Dr. Aran Atkinson. Aran, this is Sam, and he's the local pizza guru for this part of Anchorage."

Sam stood there, stunned, holding the pizza, but then he smiled brightly and extended his hand. "It's a pleasure to meet you, Dr. Atkinson! Wow, that's a long call of duty."

"It was, but I'm home now. For good."

Ruby could tell that Aran felt slightly uncomfortable. he *was* back in America for good—but home? This wasn't his home. How could he say that?

Home was where the heart was, and Ruby had the distinct feeling that this wasn't where Aran's heart was.

"You've been discharged?" Sam asked.

"Yes. I was injured overseas and I'm back now to work at the hospital. I still want to serve—just serve the good citizens of Anchorage."

Sam beamed and handed Ruby the pizza. "This is on me."

"Sam, you don't have to—"

Sam held up his hands. "No. I insist. It's my pleasure to welcome back Dr. Atkinson after sacrificing so much for our country. I'll leave you two alone. Welcome home, Dr. Atkinson."

Aran nodded.

Sam slipped away and Ruby shut the door, stunned that Sam had fallen for their ruse so easily. Usually he had a lot more questions, especially when it came to what Sam felt was his role as protector and knowledge-keeper of the neighborhood. More like gossip rather than knowledge.

And she was also stunned by the fact that she'd just scored a free pizza from him.

"I set his broken leg once and didn't even get a free pizza," she said, setting the box down on the island.

Aran chuckled. "War hero. I guess that's a perk I wasn't quite expecting. I hope it's good pizza."

"And if it's not?" she asked as she opened the box and drank in the scent of melted cheese, sausage and Italian herbs.

"I don't care if it's good or not. I haven't had a pizza in a long, long time." Aran picked up a slice and took a bite. "That's *good* pizza."

"Homemade is so much better than the big chains. There's a lot of great small restaurants throughout the north that are just Mom-and-Pop type places and they make the best food. There was this great café in Yellowknife I loved going to. It served the best Arctic Grayling sushi."

Aran cocked an eyebrow. "Arctic Grayling *sushi*?"

"Oh, yeah. Nothing quite like getting fresh Arctic Grayling right out of Great Slave Lake."

"Hey, in San Diego we have great seafood and authentic Mexican food. Not that junk you get in chain restaurants either. Have you ever had a fish taco?"

"No. I can't say that I have."

"That's a good taco."

"I'll take your word for it, since I doubt I'll ever go to San Diego." And then she mentally kicked herself, because she'd had a chance to go there and hadn't taken it.

"Never say never. You might one day."

Heat bloomed in her cheeks. "Well, I'm glad you like the pizza."

"So, you obviously told more than just the people at the hospital about me?"

"Yes. Sam has a son and he was always trying to fix me up with him. You got me out of many, many pity dates."

"Pity dates?"

"What else would you call them? Dates for

a single woman who never goes out and always works…?"

"I doubt they were pity dates, Ruby. There's so much more to you and I think they saw that."

She blushed again and looked away. She wasn't used to compliments.

They sat in silence. Ruby was tired, but she had to take Chinook down to the lake and let him have a good run or he would howl all night.

She grabbed her sweater and bear spray.

"Where are you going?" Aran asked, watching her.

"I have to take Chinook down to the lake for a swim and to stretch his legs. He needs to run off his energy. This is the problem with having a sled dog for a pet and working odd hours."

"I'll come with you, if you don't mind," Aran said.

He made his way to the guest room and came back with a flannel jacket. She noticed he was limping slightly, and was worried that the walk would be too much.

"Are you sure you're going to be okay?" she asked.

"I'll be fine. Besides, there's no backing out now. Chinook looks raring to go."

Aran nodded at the window and Ruby saw Chinook with his face against it, smearing up the outside with his nose and tongue. His blue eyes were bright with excitement.

She chuckled. "Okay, let's go before he dirties up the entire pane."

Ruby locked up and they headed outside. Chinook started barking and hopping around excitedly as she led Aran down to the path, through the forest that led to the lake. Chinook soon took off, but he never went far.

"So, if Chinook needs so much exercise, and you keep such odd hours, why did you get him?"

"No one wanted him," Ruby said. "He was supposed to be a champion dog for the Iditarod team, but he was injured on the first leg of the race. He'll never race again. If you watch him closely you can see that he has a slight limp in his giddy-up."

Aran cocked his head. "Yeah, I can see it now."

"I didn't want to see him put down, or have him waste away somewhere. The owner of the team didn't want to pay for the surgery to fix him, so I did. And he's been my pal ever since. He's well trained and he watches my place. He's happiest outside in his dog house, but on bitter nights I bring him inside. When I'm away for long periods the neighbors come and walk him, and in the winter we do some mushing down on the lake when it freezes over."

"You run a dog sled?" he asked in amazement.

"Only a small one. I like the Iditarod. It's kind of fascinating and it's a big deal up here."

"So I've heard. I've never watched it."

"You should. If you're going to stay up in Alaska you need to immerse yourself in all her excitement."

"Alaska is exciting?" he asked in disbelief.

"Yes," she said, beaming up at him.

"You told me the north is hard."

"It can be, but it's an amazing place. There's no other place I'd rather be."

There was a splash as they rounded the last bend and they saw Chinook happily splashing in the lake, barking and chasing fish. Aran chuckled and wandered down to the shore. She could tell that he was taking in the sight around him. The mountains framing the lake. The tall spruce trees. The quaking aspens rising and climbing up the mountain, each of them tall and slender, their leaves stretching as far as they could to grasp the short bursts of sunlight during the winter months, before darkness descended and the temperature was brutal.

If only he could see it in the fall and the winter, when the Aurora danced across the sky. That was her favorite time of the year. She closed her eyes and pictured the blue, green and purple lights dancing overhead. The hum that they generated in the silence of darkness...

A gunshot rang out and Chinook barked, his fur standing on end. Ruby spun around and saw Aran was completely on edge.

"What was that?" he asked.

"I—" She was just going to say that she didn't know when another shot rang out, followed by screams. Aran's jaw clenched.

"It's not hunting season," Ruby said.

She gave a quick command to Chinook and the dog came to her side. She cocked her head and listened. She could hear someone coming.

She gripped her bear spray tighter and waited. Aran was stiff as a board and his eyes were fixated on the bush behind them as the sound of someone running came closer. Chinook growled low.

Please don't be an angry bear. Please don't be an angry bear.

"Help!" A man burst through the brush, blood all over his face and hands. "Help, my buddy's been shot!"

CHAPTER FIVE

WHEN ARAN HAD heard those shots fired his heart had stopped. The world around him had frozen and his body had coiled tight, like a spring that was ready to snap. Immediately he'd been taken right back to when the fight had broken out—just before the IED explosion had injured him and wiped out his unit...

"We're under fire!"

Aran craned his head back to see the driver radioing for help. His pulse thundered in his ears and he turned back to the patient he was transporting. The soldier with the open abdomen that had now been packed. The man whose life was in his hands.

Bullets bounced off the metal, and behind him he could see a Jeep burst into flames as it hit an IED.

He trembled—and then felt the world beneath him crumble...

Seeing the confused and dazed hunter come crashing out of the bush brought him back to reality.

"Slow down and tell us where he is," Ruby said calmly.

Aran glanced down to see Chinook standing next to him. The dog was no longer growling, but he could tell he was completely on guard, his gaze focused on the distraught hunter. Or he could only assume he was a hunter, given the camo the man was wearing and the fact that they'd heard gunshots.

"He's not far away. We were in the woods hiking and Zeke thought he saw a bear."

"Okay," Ruby said. "Take us to him and we'll see what we can do, Mr….?"

"Mike," the man said breathlessly. "My name is Mike."

"Okay, Mike. Lead the way."

Mike started making his way up the trail and Ruby turned and gave Aran a strange look. Aran had the feeling that Mike and Zeke shouldn't be out hunting, especially so close to town. Chinook's hackles were still raised. The dog was on alert and Aran was thankful that he was with them.

It didn't take them long before they found Zeke, his back against the tree and holding his side. Even from this distance Aran could tell the man had a collapsed lung, just by the way he was struggling to breathe and the color of his skin.

"I found help, Zeke!" Mike said.

Aran knelt down. Ruby gave a command to her dog and Chinook immediately lay down, but he was ever watchful.

"Mind if I look?" Aran asked, before he even tried to remove the man's hand from the wound.

"You a doctor?" Zeke asked through labored breaths.

"I am."

Zeke nodded. Aran inspected the wound. He'd seen this before. Gunshot wounds were common at the front.

"Okay, Mike, do you have something like a

piece of material that you can apply pressure to?" Aran asked.

Mike nodded and dug in a rucksack, pulling out a clean shirt. "Will this do?"

"That's good." Aran took the shirt from Mike and held it against the wound. "I need you to stay with me, Zeke. I'm going to send Dr. Cloutier here to get some supplies from her house and call the paramedics."

Ruby nodded. "I know what you need."

"Good. Hurry," Aran urged under his breath.

"Chinook—come," Ruby said.

Chinook got up and followed after her.

"Am I going to die?" Zeke asked.

"Not if I can help it," Aran said. "I was at the front line and I saw guys in worse shape than you and they pulled through."

"You're Army?" Mike asked.

Aran nodded. "Yes."

He could tell they were both relieved. It gave Mike and Zeke some comfort and it would help them relax, before what Aran knew he would have to do to ensure that Zeke survived transport to the hospital. It was not going to be pretty.

"What were you out hunting for?" Aran asked.

"Well, we weren't *hunting*," Mike said quickly.

"You're certainly outfitted like you were."

"We were practicing. We're going on a hunt when the season opens. We're headed further up north, to a camp, and we're going to stalk big game. We thought we'd check out some of our gear on this trail. My summer place is just the other side of the lake. Zeke thought he saw a bear…"

"I panicked," Zeke said. "I've never hunted before."

"I think your hunting days might be over," Aran remarked.

Zeke smiled weakly. "I think you're right."

It wasn't long before Aran heard an engine and he looked down the trail to see Ruby driving a small ATV with a sled hooked to the back, like a gurney. He was impressed. She really was ready for anything out here.

"The ambulance is on its way, but the paramedics can't get out here. We need to stabilize him and then take him back slowly on the gurney."

"Good thinking." Aran glanced at Mike. "I need you to do me a favor, Mike."

Mike nodded. "Sure."

"I need you to hold this shirt and apply pressure while Dr. Cloutier and I get everything ready—okay?"

Mike looked unsure, but nodded. "Okay."

Aran showed him how to apply pressure and then let Mike take over before going to see what Ruby had brought. He was hoping she'd brought a surgical kit.

"You *did* bring the right kit," he said with relief, under his breath.

"This is not my first rodeo," she stated.

"How long until the paramedics get here?" Aran asked.

"Thirty minutes. We'll hear the sirens. The highway isn't far from here."

Aran opened the surgical kit and saw everything he needed to insert a chest tube.

"Does he really need a chest tube?" Ruby whispered, as if reading his mind.

"He has a collapsed lung and a flail chest," Aran said. "We need to do something to relieve the pressure."

"I don't have anything to sedate him. His body has been under a lot of stress, and this is going to add more."

"I'm aware," Aran said. "I've done this countless times before, in worse conditions and under gunfire. I can handle this."

Ruby didn't look so sure. "Should we get him on the gurney before we do this?"

Aran nodded. "It would be best. He won't feel like moving much after I do it."

Ruby pursed her lips together and nodded. "You get the stuff ready and I'll help him up."

Aran went through the surgical supplies and pulled out everything he needed while Ruby instructed Mike on getting Zeke strapped into the gurney.

"He's ready," Ruby said.

Aran slipped on rubber gloves and knelt down to the gurney. "Zeke, you need a chest tube. Your lung has collapsed and this will help you, but I'm not going to lie—it's going to hurt something fierce."

Zeke closed his eyes and nodded and Mike worried at his bottom lip. Aran didn't want to sugarcoat how much it was going to hurt, but the guy was young, healthy and strong. If Zeke got the help he needed then he should fully recover, but in order to get that medical attention Aran had to do this.

Now.

"Mike, I need you to help hold Zeke," Ruby instructed. "We have to keep him still while Dr. Atkinson works."

"Sure thing, Doc." Mike followed Ruby's instruction.

Aran cut away the shirt to expose the side of Zeke's chest and use an antibacterial wipe on him.

"Okay, Zeke… Hold him tight, Mike," Aran warned.

Mike closed his eyes and nodded.

Aran swiftly inserted the chest tube while Zeke screamed and cussed.

"Good job, Zeke," Ruby said gently. "Good job."

Aran taped up the chest tube and made sure it was secure.

"Dang it, Doc. That more than just hurt…" Zeke said weakly, before his eyes rolled into the back of his head and he passed out.

"He needs to get to the hospital."

"Dr. Franklin is on duty," Ruby said. "He's waiting for him."

Aran nodded. "Let's get him to the road."

They finished securing Zeke and then Ruby got on the ATV and gently pulled Zeke's gurney closer to the main road by her home. By the time they got to the road they could hear the sirens and see the ambulance coming up the road.

"You okay?" Aran asked Mike, who looked a bit pale.

"Yeah. As long as Zeke will be okay I think I'm good."

"Still, you should go with him and get yourself checked out. It looks like you hit your head," Aran said, inspecting Mike's temple, where there was a laceration.

"Okay, Doc. What about our shotguns?"

"That's for the State Troopers to take care of. They'll be here soon. They have to investigate every gunshot wound, even if it's accidental," Ruby said.

Mike nodded. "Okay."

The ambulance pulled up and the back was opened. A young man jumped out, followed by a young woman.

"Hey, Ruby!" the male paramedic said brightly.

"Hi, John," Ruby said. "Dr. Franklin is waiting for this patient. Thirty-year-old male with a gunshot wound in the upper right quadrant. Suspect flail chest and a chest tube inserted in situ."

John nodded and with his partner got Zeke off the makeshift gurney onto theirs, where they could assess him.

"This is the patient's friend, who was with him. He has a laceration and I suspect a possible concussion," Aran said. "If you could take him too?"

John nodded. "Sure thing, Dr….?"

"Dr. Atkinson—Aran Atkinson."

John's eyes widened and he looked at Ruby. "Your husband?"

Aran could see the blush bloom in Ruby's cheeks. "Yes."

John smiled brightly. "Pleased to meet you, Dr. Atkinson."

"Same." Aran nodded curtly.

The State Troopers pulled up behind the ambulance then, and Aran took a step back. Ruby went over to talk to the troopers about what had happened and where to find the firearms. Aran was still having a hard time believing that the two men were just out on a practice hike, and he hoped that they hadn't actually killed any game—because if it was off-season they would be in serious trouble.

At least that was his understanding. He knew from his father that Alaska had strict hunting laws and that it had state troopers who were game wardens and totally focused on protecting fish and wildlife in Alaska. Plus, Ruby had found them over the border of the Chugach State Park. That was another big no-no.

Aran had no idea she lived so close to the park.

Ruby came back over to him and stood next to him. "Good job back there, inserting that chest tube."

"Thank you," he said, and he was pleased to receive a compliment from her.

"You kept your wits about you out there."

He pursed his lips. He wasn't sure he'd completely kept his cool. It had been hard for him. He hadn't been in a situation like that since the front line and it had been hard—but he'd managed it.

Though right now he could do with a stiff drink, or maybe a good night's sleep. He wasn't sure. All he knew now was that he was crashing down off that adrenaline high and he didn't want Ruby to see it.

"Thanks." He scrubbed a hand over his face. "Since the paramedics have it under control, do you mind if I go lie down for a bit? I'm feeling tired. It's been a long day."

Ruby nodded and handed him her house keys. "Sure."

"Thanks."

Aran turned around and made his way up the drive to Ruby's house. His body was shaking and he was sweating, even though it wasn't particularly warm out. He had to get out of sight and get this under control before Ruby saw.

Before Ruby knew what ate away at his very soul.

Something had changed in Aran's mood after Mike and Zeke's care had been taken over by John's paramedic team. She knew that he had been in an IED explosion that had damaged his leg and got him discharged from the Army, but she couldn't help but suspect that he had some post-traumatic stress from that situation.

Who wouldn't?

When the ambulance had left the scene, and the State Troopers had collected the firearms and what they needed from her, she headed back up to her place. It was getting close to midnight, although with the presence of the sun it was hard to tell.

Once they passed the summer equinox the sun wouldn't be up so late.

Of course she didn't mind the sun so much— it was the near constant darkness in the winter that drove her slightly squirrelly. That was one thing about going to university in southern Ontario that she had appreciated. Sure, it was dark and cold in the winter, but the sun stuck around a heck of a lot longer than it did up in Yellowknife.

She fed Chinook and made sure he was snug for the night, then headed inside. The house was quiet, and she found the dishes had been done and the kitchen was cleaned up.

That was nice of him.

His door was shut, and if he was smart he was fast asleep. Which was what she should be. She had to fly then up to Whitehead tomorrow and run a surgical clinic for Lacey, the nurse practitioner there.

She finished locking up and was about to

head upstairs to her loft when she heard a low murmur of cursing that was laced with a healthy dose of pain.

She crept toward Aran's door and knocked gently. "Aran?"

"I'm fine," he snapped from the other side, but it didn't sound as if he was fine at all.

"I don't think you are."

"I am."

Ruby rolled her eyes. "I have some acet-aminophen or ibuprofen if you need it?"

She heard him groan and then move across to unlock the door. The moment he opened the door she could see the pain etched on his face. He was wearing a T-shirt and shorts and the muscles in his leg looked hard and stiff.

"Well, you might as well come in and see the mess for yourself," he said with resignation.

Ruby slipped into the room as Aran sat down on the edge of the bed. His leg was out straight. His hands were gripping the edge of the mattress so tightly that his knuckles were white.

"Do you mind?" Ruby asked as she knelt down in front of him.

He shook his head.

She reached out and touched the scars. It had been a deep wound and extensive surgical work had been on the leg. She was almost surprised that they hadn't amputated.

As if reading her mind, he said, "I wouldn't let them take it. There are pins, and I thought they would be better."

Ruby nodded solemnly and gently began to work on the tight muscle.

"That feels great," he murmured, his eyes closed.

She watched his face relax and could see the aging his work on the front line had caused him. The lines in his face, the bit of gray in his dark hair... Still, he was as handsome. She'd always thought he was handsome. If only she...

She shook that thought away. There was no *if only*. She didn't want a relationship. This fake marriage was as close as she was going to get.

"I think you overdid it out there."

Aran nodded and let out a deep breath as she worked the tight calf muscle in his leg. "I know—that's why I came back. I had a quick shower and then fell asleep—that is until the pain from my leg woke me up."

"It was a five-kilometer hike out there. That's a lot."

He cocked an eyebrow and looked at her. "You took me on a five-kilometer loop?"

"I didn't intend to, but our friends Mike and Zeke had other plans."

Aran groaned. "I didn't realize."

"Yeah, neither did I."

"That feels good," he murmured.

"You already said that," she said gently, but she was pleased that it was relaxing him.

"So I did—but it really does feel good. Thank you."

She looked up at him and caught his gaze. Those blue eyes were fixed on her. He was relaxing under her touch and her pulse quickened as he watched her. The heat crept up her neck into her cheeks and she knew that she was blushing again.

She hated that she blushed around him so much. What *was* it about him?

You're attracted to him, numbskull.

"I like it when you blush," he said.

"You…what?" She didn't look at him, kept focused on her work.

"Sorry. But from the first moment I saw you, you came off so harsh, so cold. It's nice to see this side of you."

"What do you mean?" she asked.

"That first day I showed up for my residency… I introduced myself to you and you just looked me up and down and said nothing."

"You were the competition," she teased.

"Ah, so *that's* why you were so cold."

"Exactly." She continued her massage. "You know, I like this new side of *you* too."

"How do you mean?" he asked.

"When I first met you, you were a bit of an arrogant ass."

"Was I?"

"You were the son of the president of the board of directors. You had swagger. That's another reason I was so cold to you. I thought you'd had an easy ride."

Aran chuckled. "Right. Sorry about that."

"And *I'm* sorry I assumed you were a spoiled, pompous jerk."

"Well, I was a bit arrogant."

"Just a bit." Ruby smiled and shrugged. "Well, you did me a solid. I owe you for that."

"I take payment in massages. You're quite adept at it. It feels great."

"So you said—twice," she replied.

Her pulse was racing as he closed his eyes and relaxed under her touch. She liked that she was giving him relief, but this was not keeping her distance from her convenient husband. Because that was what he was. He was her fake husband. He wasn't her real husband. Their marriage might be legal on paper, but that was it. Aran was a friend and nothing more.

A friend she was completely drawn and attracted to.

She cleared her throat and looked down at the floor. "I still think you should take some ibuprofen—and I can get you a heated pad. You need to alternate hot and cold."

Aran nodded. "That's probably for the best."

She finished up and stood. "Do you think you'll be able to fly tomorrow? A bush plane is pretty compact."

"I should be fine," he said tersely, and then he sighed. "Look, I'm sorry, but the last thing I want to do is let this keep me from my work. My work is all I have. I know that you understand that."

And she did. Her career and Chinook were all she had.

She did it to honor her father. To give to others who might not live without her help. And she could tell that was important to Aran too. After the way his leg had been pieced back together she understood why he felt he needed to work, that he couldn't give up. And she admired that. She truly did.

"I do understand that. I'll get you that ibuprofen and the heated pad for the night, so that you'll be able to accompany me up to Whitehead tomorrow morning."

Aran's shoulders relaxed. "I appreciate that, Ruby."

She nodded and slipped out of the room, shutting the door behind her. Usually she kept guys at a distance. It had been nice telling people she was married, but knowing she was not really married. Aran was a good excuse to keep men at an arm's length.

She'd had a few boyfriends when she was younger, but nothing serious because she hadn't wanted to tie herself to someone who didn't understand that her job came first. That her life living in the north and saving lives was all that mattered to her.

And she didn't want to leave anyone behind. She didn't want to leave a child or a husband to grieve over her if she died on the job.

The problem was, Aran understood that.

And that was a scary prospect indeed.

CHAPTER SIX

ARAN DIDN'T LOOK RELAXED, but he was trying his best to make himself comfortable in the cockpit of her bush plane. When he'd got up that morning he'd still been moving quite stiffly, but when she'd offered to help him he'd turned her down.

And that was okay by her.

She hadn't got much sleep because she'd thought about Aran all night. She'd thought about the way he'd looked at her, and she'd imagined what it would be like to be taken in his arms. To be kissed. To be with him the way she'd always wanted to be with him.

She'd never desired anyone like this before. It scared her how much of an effect he had on her. How he *got* her. How he understood.

But she couldn't let herself think like that. They were in a marriage of convenience. Once she'd got her Green Card and an acceptable time had passed they would get a divorce and they could both move on with their lives.

What if he stays in Alaska? That's not moving on.

She shook that thought from her mind and focused on her flight path. They were flying over the end of the tree line, where the Alaska forests gave way to the endless majestic tundra of the far north.

Aran craned his neck so he could get a better glimpse out over the horizon. "Not much further?" he asked over the mic.

"Not much further," she said. "How's your leg?"

"Stiff, but I'll be fine once I can walk around and stretch it out."

Ruby nodded and adjusted her instruments, descending a bit lower. She was getting closer to the small gravel air strip that was just outside Whitehead, a tiny community at the edge of the Beaufort Sea. She could see the sea at the edge of the horizon. Just a thin silver strip that got wider the closer they got to their destination.

The community bordered the edge of Alaska and the Yukon Territory in Canada. It was as remote as remote could be, and at the top of the world, although in Canada there were even more remote communities.

"Do you know what surgeries we're going to be doing up there?" Aran asked.

"A cholecystectomy, for sure, but I'm not sure of the others. We'll assess all who come in today. We'll see everything. That's the thing with visiting these outposts—you get a variety."

"N539BY, this is WHX. You're clear to land on the runway," the voice over the radio crackled.

"This is N539BY. Roger that, WHX. We're readying to land. Dropping landing gear," Ruby responded.

"Roger," the air traffic controller responded.

"I guess they don't get many visitors up here," said Aran.

"They get cargo planes. How else are they going to get fuel and food?"

Ruby began her checks and prepared her plane to land. She lined up with the gravel airstrip just as the wind picked up, blowing in off the Beaufort Sea.

"Whoa…" Aran muttered.

"It's okay. We'll crab it in," she teased.

"What?" Aran asked.

"Crabbing is when we go in sideways instead of straight—that way the wind won't flip the plane."

His eyes widened as she adjusted her instruments and brought the plane down sideways toward the runway, before straightening and landing with just a slight bounce as the plane ran the distance it needed to slow down. She brought the plane around toward the hangar, where a group of community members were waiting.

"Good job," Aran said.

"You were white-knuckling it a bit there!"

"Maybe…" He chuckled. "Just a bit."

"Trust me."

Aran cocked an eyebrow. "Really?"

She grinned. "Just be mindful of the bears."

"What?"

"Polar bears. It's summer. The come inland when the ice breaks up."

"Great," Aran muttered. "Is this the excitement you were talking about earlier?"

She laughed. "Just a touch of excitement mixed with caution."

Being at the top of the world meant that polar bears were often a threat in the summer months. With the ice broken up, and so far out, polar bears came inland, and there were always lookouts to make sure they didn't come too close to town.

Ruby shut down the plane and opened the pilot's door. Already the side door was open, and all the medical supplies she'd loaded up were being offloaded by Lacey's staff at the clinic.

Mitchell, an elder of the community, came forward.

"Ruby, it's good to see you again," he said.

"Glad to be back, Mitchell. Is Lacey waiting for me at the clinic?" Ruby asked.

"You bet she is." Mitchell's gaze fell on Aran. "Who is this? This isn't John or Dr. Franklin. And definitely not Lindsey, your nurse."

Mitchell was teasing her, and Aran laughed.

"No." Ruby swallowed the lump in her throat as she tried to figure out how to explain who Aran was. "This is Dr. Atkinson. New to the team, but also my…"

"I'm her husband," Aran said quickly, and smiled brightly.

"Oh! You were overseas, yeah?" Mitchell asked.

Aran nodded. "I was. But I'm home now, and looking forward to working with my wife both at the hospital and on her team."

Mitchell smiled and nodded. "Good to have you back. And good to have two surgeons here today, yeah?"

"For sure."

Ruby's stomach twisted in a knot. It was hard to tell these people she worked with so closely that she was married. She'd told them before, but now that Aran was standing here it was a little bit harder—because it was a lie. She hated lying. She hated lying to Mitchell and everyone else in Whitehead. She hated that this whole marriage was a fraud.

It doesn't have to be a lie.

She ignored that thought.

"Why don't we head to the clinic before Lacey starts to worry."

"I've got my truck. The bears have been bad this summer, so it's best we drive to the clinic—unless you have a high-velocity rifle to scare them off?"

"What?" Aran muttered under his breath. "You weren't joking, then?"

"Polar bears are dangerous predators," Ruby whispered back. "It's eat or be eaten."

"I see."

"No, you don't want to see *that*." Ruby shuddered. "That is not pretty."

"I'll take your word for it," Aran said dryly.

They followed Mitchell to his truck and Ruby was crammed between Mitchell and

Aran. She was used to being crammed into a truck with Mitchell and John, or Lacey, but she wasn't used to being flush up against Aran.

"I'm not hurting your bad leg, am I?" Ruby asked as she tried to position herself so she wouldn't hurt him.

"No, it's fine. You're nice and soft."

His blue eyes were twinkling and he smirked. She realized then that he was trying to get her goat since they weren't alone.

She rolled her eyes and tried to angle herself away from him. Aran moved and rested his arm on the back of the seat, so that he almost had his arm around her, forcing her to move into the crook of his elbow.

"Cheap move!" Ruby teased.

Aran chuckled softly as Mitchell fired up the old truck and headed away from the tiny airport and across town.

Most of the homes there were built up on stilts because of the permafrost and the tides from the Beaufort Sea. Whitehead was right on the coast, near an inlet, and there were a lot of traditional fishermen who made their livelihoods out on the water.

There weren't many vehicles in town. Most people got around via ATV in the summer or snowmobile in the winter.

Even though it was the end of June there were still patches of snow on the ground, covering up the rock and lichen that grew over the tundra this far north.

The houses were painted in bright colors, and as Mitchell drove through town people came out and waved. They were happy to see Ruby.

Whitehead was far away from any other town, but it was a friendly place. It struggled with the same issues that other places did, but Mitchell was passionate about taking care of the people.

Ruby's father had been very involved in the council and making sure that the people in her own village had what they needed. Residential school may have broken him in some ways, but in others it had taught him the meaning of keeping family and community together, of healing and making sure that everyone was taken care of. Of making sure to reclaim what was once lost.

"This is a nice place, Mitchell," Aran said, but Ruby wasn't completely sure that he meant it—because Aran came from San Diego and had told her that he preferred the south over the north.

"Thanks," Mitchell replied. "We work hard and we work to take care of each other, but there are some things we can't do—and that's why we appreciate Lacey and doctors like you and Ruby coming up here and helping us out."

Mitchell pulled up to a long building that was partly built into a side of a hill and partly on stilts. There was a long wooden ramp for wheelchairs and stretchers.

"Here we are," Mitchell announced as he opened the door and climbed out. "My boys should be along soon with the medical supplies."

"Great. Thanks, Mitchell," Ruby said.

Aran slid out and Ruby was glad to have her own personal bubble back and intact. Now, if she could just calm her nerves a bit, she would be good to tackle whatever today threw at her.

The door to the clinic opened and Lacey stepped out—with a very round belly.

Ruby's eyes widened. "You're *pregnant*?"

Lacey grinned. "About twenty-nine weeks. Over the danger zone."

Ruby gave her a hug. "I had no idea. You were away and I dealt with another nurse practitioner the last time I was here."

"I was in Anchorage for a couple months on a course, and getting checked out. I hope my replacement did good?"

"She was fine," Ruby replied. "What does Jack think about being a dad?"

Jack was Lacey's husband and the village State Trooper, who kept the peace and made sure fishing and gaming laws were respected. Also, when convicts were released they would often return to their own communities, and Jack made sure that they met the conditions of their parole. He didn't just serve White-head, but traveled by bush plane to several other communities that dotted the Beaufort Sea coast.

"He's thrilled—but he wants me back down in Anchorage to give birth. He's worried. *I'm* not worried. We have a midwife up here besides me." Lacey looked past Ruby. "Who's this?"

"This is my...my husband, Dr. Aran Atkinson."

Lacey's eyebrows shot up. "Wow!"

Ruby shook her head and Lacey covered her mouth.

"Sorry, pregnancy brain," she apologized. "It's nice to meet you finally, Aran. Ruby has told me a lot about you."

Aran cocked an eyebrow and chuckled. "Has she? It's nice to meet you too, Lacey."

"Let's get inside and I'll fill you two in on what's going to happen today."

"Sounds good."

Ruby glanced back at Aran, who was still chuckling to himself, and couldn't help but laugh. She didn't know exactly why Lacey had said that to Aran. All she had ever told her about her husband was that she was married and he was overseas, serving.

Lacey had been something of a matchmaker when Ruby had first met her. In fact, Lacey had been trying to set Ruby up with Jack—but Ruby had known the moment she'd met Jack that it was Lacey he truly wanted. Another time when her fake marriage to Aran had come in handy. Once people knew you were married they stopped trying to fix you up with every single guy in a hundred-mile radius.

The clinic was warm and quiet, but Ruby knew that wouldn't last long. As soon as the doors opened, in an hour, the clinic would be packed.

"You guys can set your stuff down in the staff lounge." Lacey pointed to a door behind the desk. "I just have to get some of the charts ready. I'll come back in ten minutes and we'll go over the day's work."

Ruby opened the door to the lounge room and peeled off her coat. Aran followed her in.

"I have a question," he said.

"What's that?"

"What exactly have you been telling people about me? I mean, everyone I've met knows exactly who I am and is excited to meet me…"

"What do you mean, what have I been telling them? I've told you what I've been saying."

"And what *is* that again?" he teased.

"That you served overseas and your name."

"That's it?" he asked, and there was the smug smirk she remembered.

"Yes. What's your point?"

"Lacey hearing 'so much' about me."

And there was another saucy smirk on his face.

Oh, Creator.

"Again, I only told her your name, the fact you were a surgeon in the Army, who your mother was, and that you were overseas. Also that we did a year of residency together."

Aran looked a bit disappointed. "That's it?" he said again.

"What else was I going to tell her?" Ruby asked, and then she lowered her voice. "I didn't tell them that our marriage was a sham and that we barely knew each other."

"We know more about each other now, after only a couple of days."

Ruby cocked an eyebrow and crossed her arms. "Oh? Enlighten me."

"You know I come from San Diego. You know that I haven't seen much of Anchorage and don't know much about the north. And you know the damage done to my leg."

"And I know you're a pretty good surgeon."

Aran smiled and his expression softened. "See? Those are things. But I was kind of hoping that you'd told some juicy lies about me."

Ruby tied back her hair into a bun and then pulled her scrubs out of her bag. "I'm not a good liar. I give this tight smile and just kind of stare off into space while I try not to sweat."

He chuckled. "Yeah, I've seen that expression before. You were wearing it the day we got married."

"What?" she asked.

Aran grinned and she laughed out loud.

"I did *not* grin like that," she said.

"You *so* did."

Ruby rolled her eyes. "I suppose I did. That was a very uncomfortable situation."

And she remembered how, even though she knew now that he had been upset about his father's death, he'd taken her hand and calmed her down, and how much she'd appreciated it.

"Agreed." He pulled out the set of scrubs he'd packed and then slipped off his shirt.

Ruby tried to not watch him as he changed, but she couldn't help it. He wasn't as ripped as he had been before he'd shipped out, but he was still a well-built specimen.

She could see scars from the shrapnel littering his side. He hadn't told her much about the IED explosion, but from the way his leg had been damaged and the scars on his torso it seemed he was lucky to have survived.

The thought of him almost dying caused her anxiety.

What if he had died? How would she have got her Green Card?

And then she felt bad for thinking so self-ishly about herself.

As if he knew she was staring, he glanced over his shoulder. "What?"

"Your scars. That must've been one of heck of an explosion."

His jaw tightened and he pulled his shirt down over his head and covered them up. "Yeah."

She'd obviously touched a sore spot and she couldn't blame him. She couldn't even begin to fathom what it would have been like and she knew that she wasn't going to press him on the matter—just as she didn't want him to press her on the matter of her father's death.

They finished getting changed in tense si-lence and Lacey came back to the room with a pile of charts.

"You two ready? Our cholecystectomy pa-tient is ready to go!"

"Yeah," Ruby said.

Aran just nodded, and then they followed Lacey out of the lounge area to start their long day of surgeries and consults.

* * *

Aran was exhausted. He hadn't pulled such a long day since before his injury. He'd done that surgery with Ruby when he'd first arrived in Anchorage, but that had been just one surgery. Then there had been the flail chest in the woods but, again, that had been one isolated incident.

It was a much different thing seeing case after case and doing many minor day surgeries to save the people of Whitehead a very expensive trip down to Anchorage or Juneau.

His leg was aching too, but there had been a lull, so he quietly slipped away and made his way back to the lounge. There was a comfortable-looking couch there, and after he'd grabbed himself a cup of lukewarm coffee he sat down and leaned his head back.

Ruby hadn't been joking when she'd mentioned that it would be tough work. Now he understood his limitations.

He'd had physiotherapy, and had been cleared to do surgery, but he should've eased himself into it rather than thinking he could just go back to the way he'd always done things.

He hated that the injury was preventing him from just getting back into the swing of things as he'd always done.

One thing that had made it easier was working with Ruby and Lacey. They both ran a tight ship and he appreciated that. Lacey's staff were well equipped to handle day surgeries and that was impressive.

It wasn't just the people in Whitehead who were utilizing the clinic today—they were flying in from all the other isolated little communities.

Lacey had handled the day-to day-appointments, while Ruby and he handled what Lacey couldn't.

"How are you holding up?" Ruby asked as she came into the room and poured herself a cup of coffee.

"A little sore, but I just need ten minutes and I'll be back at it."

Ruby leaned against the counter and took a sip of coffee. "I think we're done."

"Don't say that."

"Why?" she asked.

"Inevitably when a doctor says that there will be some crazy emergency."

Ruby chuckled softly. "Not here. No other flights are coming in and Lacey is dealing with the last of the regular check-ups."

Aran scrubbed a hand over his face. "I hope you're right."

"As soon as my last patient comes out of the post-anesthesia recovery room I'm going to suggest high-tailing it out of here. I've been watching the radar and there's a nasty storm coming down from the mountains. I'd like to get back to Anchorage tonight."

"Because of Chinook?" Aran asked.

"No, he's fine. Sam will check on him. But if it's a bad storm we could be stuck for a couple of days. The temperature has dropped outside."

"You're not seriously telling me it's a snow storm?" Aran asked in disbelief. "It's *June*."

"Yeah, exactly. It's June. Stranger things have happened."

"Okay, then, I'll go get…" Aran trailed off as Lacey came in. He could tell by her pained expression something was wrong.

"Hey, guys. It's Mitchell…"

"What about Mitchell?" Ruby asked.

"Appendicitis. It's bad. His son Max just brought him in."

"Okay." Ruby finished her coffee.

"See?" Aran said, and he finished his coffee and got up.

"You were right." Ruby stretched. "You okay to handle this?"

"I'm good. Maybe we can stabilize him with some antibiotics and fly him down to Anchorage?"

"Hopefully—and hopefully before the storm hits." Ruby tossed her coffee cup in the garbage. "You ready?"

Aran nodded. "Yeah, as ready as I'll ever be."

He followed her and Lacey as they made their way to an empty exam room. The last of the post-operative patients were being taken care of and discharged. As soon as he walked into the exam room and saw Mitchell he could tell that this appendicitis wouldn't be stopped with simple intravenous antibiotics.

The man's appendix was about to rupture.

Ruby took the chart from Lacey and shook her head gently, showing him the last recorded temperature.

"It's high," Aran said quietly.

"I did an ultrasound and the appendix is enlarged. He is unable to pass gas and his blood test shows a high white blood count," Lacey said.

"What's wrong with my dad?" Max asked.

"Appendicitis," Ruby said. "Mitchell, were you feeling this bad this morning?"

Mitchell winced. "I thought I had some indigestion, but it just got worse as the day went on."

Ruby looked at him. "Well, what do you think, Aran?"

"That appendix needs to come out before we can fly him down to Anchorage."

"My dad has to have *surgery*?" Max asked, shocked.

"Yes," Aran said. "He needs that appendix removed. If it isn't it could burst and be fatal for him."

Max nodded, but looked worried. "I should get my mom. Dad, you going to be okay?"

Mitchell nodded. "I am. Be careful, yeah?"

"I will."

Max left and Lacey began prepping a bag of antibiotics and getting Mitchell some pain medication.

"Lacey, can you prep Mitchell for surgery and we'll get the operating room ready?" Ruby asked.

"Of course, Ruby."

Aran followed Ruby out of Mitchell's room.

"I don't think we're going to beat that storm. And even if we did, I wouldn't want to risk transporting Mitchell to Anchorage this late in the evening."

"Agreed. So we stay here and hope that the weather clears in the morning?"

Ruby nodded. "There's no other choice. That appendix is going to rupture before we can get him to the hospital and that's much worse than getting stuck in Whitehead for a couple of days."

"Okay, well, let's get that appendix out." Aran winced slightly. His leg was bothering him. "I'm going to take some ibuprofen and I'll meet you in the operating room."

"Okay."

Aran headed back to the lounge to grab some medication, just so he could make it through this last surgery. As he got to the front of the clinic the light disappeared and the wind shook the building, rattling the windows as the snowstorm darkened the sky.

He'd never seen anything quite like it before. And he worried that it might be more than just a night that they were stuck in Whitehead.

CHAPTER SEVEN

RUBY WAS TRYING not worry about Aran as he stood on the other side of the operating table. She could tell that his leg was bothering him, but he was still focused on his work and she had to admire him for that.

There was a lot she liked about him. She'd forgotten what he was like. How much she'd missed him—how much she'd missed working with him.

She definitely needed his help in operating the laparoscope to remove Mitchell's appendix. Lacey was sitting next to Mitchell's head, monitoring him, and her anesthesiologist was making sure that Mitchell stayed under.

Ruby kept her attention on the screen in front of her as she navigated through Mitchell's peritoneum to find the nasty little appendix.

"There it is," Ruby said confidently.

It was red and swollen. A couple more hours and she had no doubt that it would burst. Long before they'd be able to get to Anchorage.

"Looks bad," Aran said.

Ruby nodded and adjusted the laparoscope so she could remove the appendix and invert the stump into the cecum. "With the storm raging outside, there's no way we would've made it to the hospital. I'm wondering how long he's been masking his symptoms…"

"I don't know," Lacey piped up. "He's pretty good at hiding things like this. He doesn't ever want to be a bother and he doesn't want to take off time from work."

"Ah, that sounds like Mitchell for sure."

Ruby finished removing the appendix and sealing off the wound. Mitchell would still have to go down to Anchorage and be on intravenous antibiotics for a few days, to make sure that no abscess formed and he didn't get a post-operative infection. Post-operative infections were uncommon, but with something like the appendix Mitchell would have to be closely monitored.

Aran took over to help remove the instruments and close up the wound.

"Good job, Doctors," Lacey said. "I am *beat*."

"You need to rest," Ruby remarked as she cleaned up.

"Yes. Thankfully Joanna the night nurse will be on duty soon, to monitor all the patients and be here in case of any post-operative complications."

"We'll be here too," Ruby said. "We're not flying out in this weather. Is there a couple of rooms we can use for the night?"

Lacey gave her a strange look. "A couple of rooms? Don't you two want the same room?"

Ruby's heart skipped a beat and she could see Aran's spine stiffen as he finished bandaging Mitchell.

"Oh...yeah, right. I'm just tired." It was an excuse but she hoped that Lacey bought it. "One room is all we need."

"I understand that," Lacey remarked as she

made some notes on Mitchell's chart. "Besides, we only have one extra room at the moment. Good thing you two are married!"

"Yeah, good thing…"

Ruby glanced at Aran. He wasn't looking at her, but she could tell by the way his body had tensed that he wasn't exactly thrilled with the prospect of sharing a room with her. She only hoped it had a set of bunks or a couple of beds, like on-call rooms usually had.

After they'd finished with Mitchell, and made sure that he was stable in the post-anesthesia recovery unit, with Joanna the night nurse and Mitchell's wife Kayla, Lacey showed them to the room that was used for locum medical staff.

"It's a small room, but it has a double bed."

Lacey opened the door and Ruby's heart sank when she saw how tiny the room was. The double bed filled the small space. There really would be nowhere to escape Aran. And if someone found him or her sleeping on the couch in the lounge they would question why they weren't sleeping together.

It's only sleeping.

They had slept in the same on-call room before.

Yeah, but you never shared a bed with him.

"This is great. Thank you," Aran said cordially.

Lacey nodded. "I'm just down the hall. With Jack out of town I'd rather stay close to the clinic."

"That's a good plan," Aran replied, because Ruby was clearly still too stunned to say anything.

"Night!"

Lacey turned and headed down the hall. When she was out of sight Ruby groaned.

"What're we going to do?" Ruby asked.

Aran ushered her into the room and shut the door, closing it behind him. "What do you mean, what're we going to do? We're going to lie down and try and get some sleep so that we can transport Mitchell to Anchorage tomorrow."

"We have to share a *bed*!"

"So?" Aran asked.

"We've never done that before!"

"We're married," Aran stated.

"Yeah, but still…" Ruby rubbed her temple. "I'm freaking out over this."

"Why?" he asked. "You're safe with me."

"I know. I just hate all this deception. I hate this immigration interview looming. I hate it all."

"I know," he said softly. "Me too."

"I know…sorry. I'm tired."

"We both are."

Aran glanced down at the small double bed, which was placed up against the wall. There was just enough space to walk in and out of the room. That was it. It was a place for people to rest their heads at night. Nothing more.

"Which side do you want?" he asked.

"I think, given your leg, you should have this side. You're, like, six foot, and you're going to need extra space. I'm more compact at five-five. I can cram into the corner."

Aran looked relieved. "Thanks. I didn't particularly feel like cramming myself anywhere."

AMY RUTTAN 159

Ruby kicked off her shoes and then crawled across the creaky bed and tried to make herself somewhat comfortable before Aran got in.

"You ready?" he asked.

"As ready as I'll ever be."

He chuckled and sat on the edge of the bed to remove his shoes. Then slowly he lay down, trying to stretch out his sore leg.

Ruby giggled.

"What?" he asked.

"Your foot touches the door and your head is at the wall!"

Aran craned his neck to look and then shrugged. "I've slept in tighter spots than this."

The wind howled outside. It was a deafening sound as it hit the corrugated steel buildings and whipped across the tundra.

Aran shuddered. "A snowstorm in June..." he mumbled.

"Get used to it," Ruby replied.

"It sounds a bit like a sandstorm, to be honest. Had a few of those when I was serving. At least snow melts—sand just gets into everything. Even the patients you're working on."

"I can't even imagine."

"Don't try. It's awful."

Ruby couldn't sleep. All she could do was stare up at the ceiling and count the marks on it. She knew Aran was awake too, because of the way he was breathing. It wasn't steady and even. And his body was still tense, as if he was trying to give her space.

"I think I prefer snow," she said, breaking the tension.

"What?" he asked.

"Well, as you say, snow melts. Sand stays and shifts around. It never leaves. Although there are times in the winter when the top layer of snow blows and shifts like the desert. You get white-out conditions—not because it's fresh snow, but blowing snow when there's no trees to break it."

"That would be neat to see."

"Not if you're driving in it."

She remembered the few times her older brother had had to stop on the highway between Yellowknife and Enterprise because the snow had been bad. He always had emergency gear in the back and he always knew the good places to stop.

Their father had taught him that. Taught him how to survive. Because he had run away from residential school. He'd been lucky to make it when so many didn't. Her dad had been going to show her too, but he'd never got around to teaching her. He'd died before he got the chance.

So she'd taken it upon herself to learn. She'd taken it upon herself to learn a lot of things. All the things her father had promised to teach her.

And now, as she thought about her father, all she could see was his body on that cold metal table. His eyes closed, no life left in him. Just an empty shell.

No.

She was not going to think about that. Not here.

"I could survive a snowstorm, but not sand," she said offhandedly, breaking the tension and trying to shoo away the memories of her father.

"You've taken survival courses?" he asked, intrigued.

"To live and work in remote areas you need to. You need to know how to survive on the land."

"We took some as part of our training. But I wouldn't mind a refresher on surviving here in the winter."

"I can show you," she offered, pleased that he wanted to learn. She'd always thought of him as a soft southerner, but maybe she was wrong. He was proving to be anything but the spoiled, privileged, arrogant man she'd thought he was when she'd first met him all those years ago.

"Would you?"

"Of course. If you're going to be part of a medical team, you need to know."

He turned and looked at her. His face was so close to hers.

"Thank you."

"No problem." She stifled a yawn.

"You should try to sleep. *I* can't fly the plane tomorrow."

She smiled. "I know. I'm just not used to sharing a bed with anyone."

"I'm not used to this constant daylight. Although the storm helps to darken the room a bit."

"You get used to it. It's why I have blackout blinds."

"I still can't sleep. I'm exhausted, but…"

He trailed off and then turned his head away. She could tell that something had changed. That he'd been going to say something and thought better of it.

It's not your business.

Although she couldn't help wonder what it was. She didn't want to pry. Well, she *did* want to pry, but she wasn't going to. She couldn't get involved with him. Sure, he was her husband, but it was just until she got her Green Card.

Still, there was a part of her that wanted to know more about him. There was a part of her that was comfortable being around him. She hadn't been as lonely since he'd shown up. It was nice having someone to talk to instead of Chinook.

"Count sheep?" she suggested.

"That never works."

"How do you know? Have you tried?"

He glanced back at her. "No—have you?"

"No."

"Then why would you suggest it?"

Ruby shrugged. "Everyone suggests it."

"So, that makes it a certainty that it will put me to sleep?" he teased.

"No, but it's been common knowledge for a long time. Sheep are kind of boring, right?"

"Why are we having a conversation about sheep?" he asked.

"I don't know—probably because you won't stop talking."

"Sorry about that." He groaned and rubbed his eyes.

"I can't sleep either," she said. "I'm tired, but I really can't sleep. I'm not used to sleeping next to someone."

"So you keep saying."

"Sorry." Heat bloomed in her cheeks. "Not even Chinook sleeps with me."

Aran rolled over and propped himself on one elbow. "You've never lived with anyone?"

"My parents and siblings. And I had a roommate in university, but we didn't share a bed."

"No, I mean…a boyfriend or a fiancé or some other significant other?"

Heat bloomed in her cheeks. "I've had boyfriends, but never long-term. So, no, I've never slept in the same bed as anyone."

Ruby was not used to talking so intimately with someone. Not even with her girlfriends. And she didn't have many of those because her career was her life. She didn't make much time for her friends, and eventually some of those friends had stopped inviting her to places.

Even if she did go out, she didn't really open up about her life. Keeping to herself was a way to compartmentalize her feelings, so she could keep focused on her work. It was why any relationships she'd had had never lasted.

Men said she wouldn't open up. That she was too focused on her work.

It had never really bothered her.

Until now.

"You're blushing again," he said softly.

"I don't talk about my personal life."

"I remember. You were always all business. Which is why I liked you so much."

"Right…"

Her heart had fluttered when he'd said he liked her.

Don't think about it. You're friends. That's all.

"Why did you like me," she asked, "if I was all business? I saw you with others…you know…before we were married."

"You were driven and focused. I admired that. And, to be honest, I thought you were a challenge I wanted to take on. I don't think that way now."

"A challenge?" she asked, annoyed.

"Yeah, but once I got to know why you were so focused and what you wanted to do I didn't think that way anymore. You were not just someone I wanted to conquer. I learned that lesson fast. Instead I wanted to be a part of your work."

Her heart skipped a beat again.

You're treading on dangerous ground.

She couldn't let him get too close. She had to keep him at a distance. But it was nice lying here in bed and talking to him. To have this moment of connection.

"I should know some personal facts before this Agent Bolton comes and talks to us," he said.

"If I open up are you going to open up?"

"Sure. If I think you need to know," he stated.

"Ditto."

"So how do we do this?" he asked.

"We play fifty questions."

His eyes widened. "Fifty?"

"Or the amount of questions until we get bored and/or fall asleep."

Aran sat up and she did too. They were sitting cross-legged across from each other.

"What do we start with?" he asked.

"Favorite color?"

"Green," he said. "Yours?"

"Red. Now you ask a question."

"I don't know…" He ran his hand through his hair, as he often did when he didn't know what to say or was annoyed.

"Just think of one," she said.

"Uh… I'm not good at this. I don't want to do this."

"This was your idea, pal. You wanted to get to know me."

He ran his hand through his hair again. "What drink would you be?"

She looked at him like he was crazy. "What *drink* would I be? Don't you mean what drink do I like?"

"No, what drink would you *be*. If you weren't human, what drink would you be?"

Ruby sat there, stunned. And then she saw a strange smirk on his face. She flicked him on his good knee.

"Ow—what was that for?" he asked.

"That's a stupid question."

"No question is stupid." His eyes were twinkling.

"That one was."

Aran laughed softly. "Sorry."

"I don't know how we're going to convince this Agent Bolton that we've been properly married for five years and that we know each other well—especially when we can't seem to relax around each other. The only time we're relaxed is in surgery, and I hardly think Agent Bolton will want to do his interview in the operating room."

"I know one way," Aran said softly.

Her pulse began to race. "Oh?"

"Well, we can kiss and break the tension that way."

Say no. Say no.

"Okay."

Her voice went up one octave as she said it. What was she thinking? This was a bad idea.

Except she was curious. She was attracted to him and she had always wondered what it would be like to kiss him—just once. And he was right. It might ease the tension between them.

"You sure?" he asked.

She nodded. "You're right. We have to be more comfortable around each other and a kiss is a pretty easy way to do that. Let's do it."

"Relax," he whispered, and he reached out and touched her face.

Just the simple touch made her stomach flip-flop with anticipation.

"I'll try." But she couldn't look at him, and she was sure that her cheeks were bright red. She'd kissed guys before—what was so different about this?

You're not in control.

Aran inched closer to her and tilted her chin so she was forced to look at him. She wanted to look away, but she couldn't.

"It's okay," he whispered.

Ruby relaxed, mesmerized by him. His gentle touch was electric, igniting every nerve-ending under her skin. Her heart hammered against her chest.

With that simple acknowledgement that it would be okay he'd cast a spell over her. So much so she felt she was losing control—something she usually kept a tight rein on.

But she didn't care.

It was okay.

He cupped her face, his thumbs brushing her cheeks, and no matter how much the rational side of her wanted to fight it, she couldn't. For the first time in her life Ruby gave over control to a man, when *she* was usually the initiator of any intimate moments. This time she just reveled in the sensation, in the desire that Aran was stirring in her.

She closed her eyes and let him kiss her. His lips were gentle against hers. And then the kiss deepened and she welcomed it. It had been so long since she had been kissed by a man or had any kind of physical connection with another person.

It was intoxicating. The simple act of human contact with a man she desired was creating a hunger, a need to have more.

Aran wrapped his arms around her and she forgot everything else as she melted against him. In that brief moment he made her feel safe...he made her feel alive.

What are you doing?

As his hands moved down her back she realized this was dangerous territory. She pushed him away. "I can't. We can't...not here."

"You're right," he murmured, and pulled away. "I'm sorry. I... I'm sorry."

"Don't be sorry. It was nice."

He nodded. "Yeah..."

She bit her lip. Her body wanted more, and her pulse was still racing, but this was not the place to do anything more than kiss.

Aran stood.

"Where are you going?" she asked.

"I need to take a little walk, and then I'll do a round on the patients. You rest."

Before she could stop him he'd opened up the door and slipped out into the hallway.

Ruby lay down. There was no way she was getting any sleep now. Not with the taste of Aran on her lips, her blood thrumming in her veins and her body craving more than just a simple kiss.

CHAPTER EIGHT

ARAN TOOK A long walk to try and calm down. He had wanted to kiss Ruby for a long time, although he'd never intended for it to go that far. But the moment he'd tasted her sweet lips he'd just wanted more.

What were you thinking?

It was taking all his willpower not to go back to her and throw himself at her feet. He was attracted to her.

Usually when he was attracted to someone he saw them a few times and then it was done. The romance had run its course.

Women didn't understand his devotion to his work and that was fine by him. He didn't want to be tied down. He didn't want a family only to have it broken.

And he was too broken himself.

The problem with Ruby was that she did understand his devotion to work. That was her passion too and that made him want her even more. She was smart, funny, strong, beautiful and independent. There was so much he loved about her.

He liked working with her and he wanted her. He'd always wanted her.

What was supposed to have been a simple kiss to break the tension had turned into something he hadn't expected. Something he hadn't prepared for mentally or emotionally. It had woken something inside him.

He'd thought maybe the kiss would break him of the hold she had on him, but he'd been so wrong. It had fired his blood. Made him feel alive. It had made him feel as if he was his old self again.

But he wasn't. He would never be the same person he was before. That IED explosion had shattered him. It had broken him. And Ruby deserved so much better than the pieces of him that were left.

He'd taken a walk so that she could get some rest and be able to fly them out of Whitehead if the weather had cleared in the morning. He sincerely hoped that it would.

He went back to the room and quietly opened the door. Ruby had curled up in the middle of the bed and was sleeping soundly. A smile tugged at the corner of his mouth. She looked so peaceful.

Good.

She needed the rest. It had been a long, busy day and flying up to Whitehead from Anchorage had meant that they'd started early. Ruby had definitely clocked up over eighteen hours and she needed sleep.

He was okay. He was tired, and a bit sore, but there were many nights when he couldn't sleep. When his PTSD was working in overdrive and the nightmares just wouldn't stop. He could sleep later. He didn't have to fly a plane back.

She looked so peaceful there and he wished that he could hold her.

He wished he could do more.

You need to back away.

He shut the door. The couch in the lounge

room would be the perfect place to crash. If anyone asked he'd just tell them Ruby snored.

Aran chuckled silently to himself, thinking about how Ruby would react to that. He headed into the lounge and stared at the couch.

You've slept on worse.

"Dr. Atkinson?"

Aran spun around to see the night nurse, Joanna, standing behind him.

"Yes?"

"It's Mitchell. He's spiked a fever and I can't get it to go down. I've given him the maximum amount of antibiotics I can."

"I'll be right there."

Joanna nodded and Aran washed his hands in the lounge's sink and took a deep breath to calm his nerves. He wasn't a stranger to post-operative infection and fever. Especially in situations where the wounded patient was maxed out on medication and they were waiting for transport.

He just hoped that this storm would clear so they could get Mitchell down to the larger hospital which would have access to different kinds of antibiotics and a larger staff on call. He was glad that Whitehead was equipped to deal with small surgeries, but some things were better left to a hospital.

He'd learned from working on the front line that some things just couldn't be done, and that was when you just basically did what you could to keep your patients alive until they could be shipped out. Even that was a case of throwing the dice...

He walked into the room and saw that Mitchell's heart-rate was up. He was pale and looked as if he was having trouble breathing.

"Did you run a culture of his blood?" Aran asked as he pulled out his chart.

"I did. His white cell count isn't elevated that high. He's feverish, but I don't think it's sepsis."

"I agree," Aran said.

He set the chart down and examined the wound. It was healing well and there was no sign of infection there. He moved back the sheet and saw red in Mitchell's legs. It was warm to the touch.

"Look at this, Joanna. What do you see?"

Joanna leaned in and examined it. "Deep vein thrombosis?"

Aran nodded. "Could be. Does Mitchell have a history of blood clots?"

"Not, Mitchell—but his mother did. She died of a pulmonary embolism three years ago."

"Do you have a Doppler?" Aran asked.

"We do."

Joanna left the room and Aran monitored Mitchell's pulse-rate. It was high, and Aran had no doubt that what Mitchell had was thrombophlebitis. And since they didn't have a CT scanner here the Doppler would have to do. If it was a pulmonary embolism they would have to get him back to Anchorage to do an angiogram.

Aran hoped that Whitehead stocked a supply of heparin. If he could get some heparin into Mitchell that would at least help until they got back to Seward Memorial.

Joanna returned with the Doppler.

"Here you are, Dr. Atkinson. The weather looks to be clearing. Not much snow has stayed—it's been pretty much blown away and the temperature is rising."

"Good—because we really need to get Mitchell down to Anchorage."

Mitchell moaned, but he was pretty much out of it—which was good. The poor guy had been through the wringer today, and all while putting on a smile. Aran would never understand that—hiding symptoms—but then he knew there were people out there who thought every ache was cancer. Still, the pain Mitchell must have been in would have been more than just a slight ache.

"Do you have any heparin here in Whitehead?" Aran asked.

Joanna nodded. "Of course."

"Good. Can you ready a dose, please?"

"Right away, Doctor."

Joanna disappeared out of the room again and Aran prepped the Doppler to examine Mitchell's leg. The more Aran thought about it the more he realized that the Medevac should be called in.

Ruby had the means to transport their patient, but with a deep vein thrombosis and a family history of pulmonary embolism the last thing Aran wanted was to take a risk flying Mitchell in Ruby's plane.

The larger Medevac would have more staff. It was a helicopter, and it would get Mitchell where he needed to be with the right stuff on board.

Joanna returned with the dose of heparin— and it was at that moment that Aran found the clot in Mitchell's leg.

"Thank you, Joanna. We need to get a hold of the Medevac. This can't wait until Dr. Cloutier can fly him down. He has to get out of here *now*."

"I'll call them, Dr. Atkinson. And Mitchell's wife too."

"Thank you. I'll stay with him."

Joanna nodded and Aran administered the dose of heparin, hoping that it would help until the nearest Medevac could get in to

Whitehead and take Mitchell to a hospital that would help him.

Even if it wasn't Seward Memorial.

Ruby woke with a start.

The room was brighter, but she realized that she was sleeping in the middle of the bed and that Aran wasn't in the bed with her. She sat up and looked on the floor, the small little laneway from the door to the bed. Thankfully he wasn't there either.

So I didn't knock him to the floor. That's good.

She tied back her hair and then glanced at her watch. It was nine in the morning. She'd slept way past her alarm.

Ruby scrambled out of bed and pulled the blinds. There was melting snow, blue skies and sunshine. At least the runway would be clear and they would be able to fly back to Anchorage. She was just mad at herself for being late. She *never* slept in.

She cursed under her breath, annoyed, but pulled herself together, slipped on her shoes and headed out into the hall. The clinic was quiet, but it was Saturday so that wasn't unusual. She found Aran in a waiting room chair, his head on his hand and sleeping.

Lacey rounded the corner. "You're awake!"

"I didn't mean to sleep in," Ruby said. "Sorry."

"Aran said to let you sleep. That you needed it."

Ruby glanced at Aran. He looked completely uncomfortable in that chair. "How long has he been there?"

"About an hour. He was up waiting for the Medevac to come and take Mitchell to Juneau."

Ruby's eyes widened. "Juneau? I was supposed to fly him down to Anchorage."

Lacey sighed. "Mitchell developed a post-operative fever last night that Joanna was unable to bring down with ibuprofen or antibiotics. His pulse-rate increased and she was worried. She found Dr. Atkinson leaving your room and asked for help. He found thrombo-phlebitis in Mitchell's leg and, given the family history of pulmonary embolism, he felt it would be better if the Medevac helicopter came and took him. There's another storm rolling in—this time off the Bering Sea. It's headed straight for Anchorage, so the Medevac decided on Juneau."

"Oh..." Ruby glanced at Aran.

She was annoyed that Mitchell—*her* patient—had been sent away without her knowing and that he wasn't going to be at Seward, where she could continue to monitor him, but she completely understood why Aran had done what he had.

Mitchell would need to be monitored in case the blood clot in his leg broke off and headed to his lungs or heart, which would be fatal. Medevac had more team members with them then she did. In the same shoes, she would have done the same thing.

"Kayla, Mitchell's wife, couldn't go on the Medevac so she's hoping you can take her to Anchorage. Her sister lives there, and from there they'll travel to Juneau."

"Of course. Can you let her know that I'm

leaving within the next hour? As soon as I get my flight plan logged."

"I will. And thanks again." Lacey headed back to the exam rooms.

Ruby took a deep breath and leaned against the wall.

Why hadn't Aran woken her? How had she slept through the Medevac team coming?

She felt guilty that she'd let Mitchell down. That she hadn't been the one to make the call. She'd known Mitchell for five years. She'd treated him for other ailments and she'd been the one to try and help his mother before the pulmonary embolism had killed her so suddenly. She felt bad that she'd slept through all this.

She hated losing control.

She hated that she hadn't been awake.

She hated that Aran had totally thrown her world upside down.

"Hey…" she said gently, leaning over and nudging him.

Aran jumped with a start and Ruby jumped back, surprised by his response. His eyes were wild, and for one brief moment it looked as if he didn't know where he was. As if he was on the defensive.

"Aran, it's just me."

It took a minute or so, but his wide eyes narrowed and his body relaxed. "Sorry," he said and covered his face with his hand. "Sorry. I guess I was… I was sound asleep."

There was an edge to his voice and she didn't quite believe that she had just startled him. It was something more than being startled. There was panic, a fear just behind his eyes. As if he had post traumatic stress disorder.

She wouldn't be surprised, given his experience with the IED explosion.

"So Mitchell was flown to Juneau?" she asked.

Aran stifled and yawn and nodded. "Yes. I'm sorry, but he had to be sent out of here to get proper help."

"I understand. I just wish you'd woken me up."

"Why?" he asked. "I could handle it."

"He was *my* patient."

Aran stood up. "I understand, but it's all taken care of."

"I know—and you did the right thing. Just next time wake me up and let me know."

"Wait," he said. "You're bothered?"

"I would've liked to have known."

"And what would waking you have done? He still would have had to be transferred out, with a larger team who could take him to a proper hospital. Once I gave the Medevac team an update they took over. All I did was stay up and wait for them."

"I still would've liked to have known," Ruby said sternly.

Aran shook his head. "You really don't like relinquishing control, do you?"

"He was my patient. I am the leader of this team…"

"I did right by *your* patient, and now he's off to a better facility. I don't know why you're picking a fight. If it's about last night…"

"It's not," she said quickly, but it was. She was picking a fight because she'd been so afraid at how close he'd gotten to her. How he had affected her. How his kiss had made her forget all the rules she'd put in place when it came to relationships.

She didn't want anything except casual, and there was no way you could do *casual* with someone you worked with. Getting involved with the man who was your convenient fake husband was also not casual, and she didn't want to get involved with Aran when their marriage wasn't even real and had a time limit.

Ruby understood the idea of sharing that kiss, but really it had been a bad idea all around and she shouldn't have let it happen.

"We have to get back to Anchorage. The weather has cleared and we're going to take Mitchell's wife down so she can get a flight to Juneau."

She didn't wait for a response from him— just turned on her heel and left to get everything ready. She had to call in her flight plan and have someone get the plane prepared. She had to gather up what gear was left and make sure Lacey had arranged for someone to get them to the airport.

She didn't have time to deal with the emotional crisis that Aran had stirred up in her.

She didn't have time for any of it.

She only had time for her work.

The flight back to Anchorage was somewhat awkward. Ruby felt bad that Kayla had to be a part of it, but Kayla was mostly worried about Mitchell in Juneau and the flight down to Anchorage. Ruby knew that Kayla hated flying, and that she rarely left Whitehead, but thankfully the flight was relatively smooth.

When they landed in Anchorage, Kayla's sister was waiting at the airport in the charter terminal, near where Ruby stored her plane. Ruby told Kayla to give Mitchell a big hug and said that she'd see them soon enough.

Then it was just her and Aran.

As they walked out to her truck she felt bad for the way she had treated him. She felt bad for trying to pick a fight with him. He'd done the right thing, and if the situations were reversed she would have done the same.

She'd just been scared.

"I'm sorry," she said after he'd climbed into the passenger side.

"For what?" he asked.

"For snapping at you about Mitchell. You did the right thing. And you're right—I like control. I hate losing it, and I hate when I'm not involved with my patient's diagnosis from beginning to end. But there are some things I *can't* do, and it's hard for me to let my patient's care fall into the hands of other competent surgeons. So I'm sorry."

His eyebrows arched. "Thank you. Apology accepted."

Ruby nodded. "We should get to the hospital. I was supposed to start rounds three hours ago."

"Yes… Well, I was supposed to start in the middle of the night, but look how that turned out."

Ruby started the truck and headed out on the highway to Seward Memorial. The weather was bad in Anchorage, but at least it wasn't snow. Just rain.

It was a short drive to the hospital, and when they got there Jessica was waiting for them. Ruby was surprised to see her when they got off the elevators from the main entrance to the trauma floor.

"There you two are!" Jessica said impatiently.

Ruby could tell that she was completely agitated and she saw that Aran's spine had stiffened, his body tensing in light of his mother's anxious behavior.

"I sent you a message. A storm waylaid us in Whitehead," Ruby responded calmly.

"I know," Jessica replied. "And I completely understand that. The thing is the U.S. Citizen and Immigration Services *doesn't*. Agent Bolton has been here since this morning and he's a bit annoyed that you're not here."

"Agent Bolton?" Ruby asked. "I told him to send me some dates to set up a time. He didn't."

"This is a surprise visit," Aran said. "I've heard of them before."

"Well, he's in the boardroom—waiting. You two need to go meet with him."

Ruby's stomach twisted in a knot.

Oh, Creator. How am I going to handle this?

"It'll be okay," Aran said calmly. "We'll present a united front. Just don't plaster that fake smile on your face like you did on our wedding day."

Ruby chuckled nervously. "I'll try not to."

"What fake smile?" Jessica asked.

"This one."

Ruby plastered on the smile which had been on her face the day she'd married Aran. The smile that she so often used when she was in an uncomfortable situation. Aran was laughing silently to himself and shaking his head, but Jessica looked less than impressed.

"You two have to pull it together!" Jessica snapped. "This is serious."

"I know," Ruby murmured.

It was a huge risk for all of them. She should

never have agreed to it in the first place. She should have said no to Aran.

Only when she'd said yes she had heard her father's voice telling her to say yes, and she'd just closed her eyes and taken the plunge into the unknown.

Jessica pursed her lips together. "Just try and keep it together."

Ruby nodded and Jessica stormed away. "This was a bad idea," she whispered. "I thought our marriage was a good idea at the time. I wanted to stay in the country. But I shouldn't have said yes."

Aran sighed. "I asked you because I wanted to do it for you. I believed in your work. I still do believe in your work. This isn't all your fault. We both agreed to this and we'll face this together."

"Right," Ruby agreed. She took a deep calming breath and stared at the door. "We can do this."

"We can." He took her hand. "Come on, Mrs. Atkinson."

"That's *Dr.* Mrs. Atkinson, buster," she teased, and Aran laughed.

His blue eyes were twinkling and it reassured her. He took her hand, just as he had on their wedding day, and it calmed her.

Aran opened the door to the boardroom and Agent Bolton, who had been pacing by the coffee table, stopped and turned. He didn't look particularly threatening. He was a man in his mid-fifties, in a suit, and he looked like someone you could trust—which was probably exactly what he needed to look like.

Someone you could really open up to.

Someone who was good at catching lies.

It'll be okay.

She and Aran were friends. They weren't strangers. There was some intimacy. They were in this together.

Though she still really didn't completely understand why he'd done it.

Don't think about it. Focus.

"Dr. Atkinson and Dr. Cloutier, I presume?" Agent Bolton asked.

"Yes," Ruby answered. "Sorry to have kept you. We weren't expecting you."

Agent Bolton smiled, but she could tell that the smile was not sincere. It was business, and it was calculated.

"That's fine. We do like to do preliminary surprise checks on our applicants before the official interview. I thought you two would be here in the city. Not up near the Canadian border."

"You mean in Whitehead?" Aran asked.

"Yes," Agent Bolton said. "Whitehead is not far from the Yukon—where your wife is from."

"No, Ruby is from the Northwest Territories. Behchokǫ̀. Which is, I believe, near Yellowknife and one territory over."

Ruby breathed an inward sigh of relief at Aran's quick thinking.

Agent Bolton grinned again. "So it is. Why don't we have a seat?"

Aran pulled out a chair for Ruby and she sat down. She could feel her palms sweating and was glad when Aran put himself between her and Agent Bolton.

Agent Bolton looked unassuming and friendly, but right now Ruby was not a fan of his, and she was pretty sure that he wasn't a fan of hers.

"What were you two doing in Whitehead anyhow?" Agent Bolton asked.

"I was making my quarterly visit to a clinic up there. They have a nurse practitioner, but I fly my team in with me and we do all the medical procedures the nurse practitioner can't. I usually only go up there for a day, but a storm hit after I'd had to perform an emergency appendectomy and it wasn't safe to fly."

Agent Bolton nodded. "How admirable of you. That patient has been transferred here?"

"Juneau," Aran said. "During the night the nurse on call asked me to come and check on him. As my wife is the pilot, and needed her sleep, I ascertained that the patient had developed a blood clot and called for the Medevac service to transport him to the nearest hospital."

"It's a good thing that storm hit, then," Agent Bolton remarked.

Ruby gritted her teeth. She didn't like the way this agent was operating. "A very good thing," she said.

He nodded and opened the folder that sat on the table. "I have your file, Dr. Atkinson, about your service here for the last five years. Five years is a long time for a newly married couple to be apart, don't you think?"

"Yes," Ruby answered. "We wanted to marry because we were in love."

"Right," Aran said. "I didn't want to leave my girlfriend behind when I shipped out, so I made her my wife. She understood that I needed to serve my country, and she was focused on her career here."

"How long was it before you decided to get married?" he asked, and he looked at both of them.

"We dated for a year," Aran said.

"A year?" Agent Bolton asked.

"We were surgical residents together. It's how we met." Ruby smiled at Aran. "You grow close to a person when you work a forty-eight-hour shift together."

Aran grinned back at her, making her pulse slow. It was calming and reassuring.

"As soon as I knew I was going to get shipped out I asked her. I wanted her to be my wife. Sometimes you just know—and I knew. I knew from the moment I met her that she was the one."

Ruby's stomach did a flip-flop and she blushed.

Agent Bolton nodded. "But a long-distance relationship? That doesn't always work."

"I know," Aran answered. "It didn't work for my parents, but for me it was right. Ruby loves it here in the north. She's from the north, and I completed my training at Fort Irwin in San Bernardino."

"I thought you were from San Diego?" said Agent Bolton.

"My father is from San Diego, and I grew up there. My mother lives in Anchorage and I visit her here—but I'm sure you have my military records and can see where I completed my basic training."

Agent Bolton shut his folder. "Okay, then. Well, I won't take up more of your time right now. I'll come back in a week and we'll do separate interviews then, and a joint interview before I determine whether or not a Green Card will be issued to Dr. Cloutier."

Ruby stood, and Aran did as well.

Agent Bolton got up and shook their hands. "See you both next week. I'll call and arrange a day, so you two won't be off on a jaunt somewhere in the bush. Good evening, doctors."

Ruby watched him leave the boardroom and when he was gone sank down into her chair, resting her head in her hands.

"Whew! That guy was intense," said Aran.

"So it wasn't just me that was unnerved by him?" Ruby asked.

"No. He's good at his job."

Ruby shuddered. "I thought he might be a serial killer or something."

Aran chuckled. "No. He's probably got ex-military, though. It wouldn't surprise me if he's a Marine, or something like that. Most of those agents have military training."

"Well, we should go home and talk about next week." She didn't want to say too much because she was suddenly feeling slightly paranoid that the boardroom might be bugged. "Besides, I need my own bed tonight."

"Agreed."

They got up and left the boardroom in silence. She was still trembling when they walked down the hall toward the attendings' lounge. As much as she wanted to go home and formulate a plan, she was still on duty. She had to calm down so that she could focus on her patients.

It was for them that she was doing this.

It was for her patients—for all the lives that could be saved because of her work. Just like Mitchell. He had a fighting chance because she had been there to do his appendectomy. Aran had given him a further chance by being there and finding that thrombophlebitis. Because of their work Mitchell was in Juneau and alive.

Even though she was scared about what had just happened with Agent Bolton, and about having to see him again, she was glad she'd done it.

If she wasn't here to help, who would?

No one had been there to help her father when he'd needed it the most.

She was not going to let that happen to another family.

She was not going to let anyone die if she could help it.

Even if it meant faking a marriage to a man who made her want to lose control completely.

It was close to midnight when Ruby and Aran finally stumbled back to her house. Sam had taken Chinook over to his place and left a note, but Ruby was tired and it was too late to go over there and get him. She just wanted to sleep in her own bed and try to forget about the events of the last couple of days.

"I think before we go to sleep we should

figure out our story," Aran said as he took off his shoes.

"Really? I'm exhausted. I've flown down from Whitehead. Been grilled by a government agent. And worked a five-hour shift at the hospital."

"I'm tired too, Ruby, but we need to strategize. I don't know why you insisted on waiting so long to talk about it."

"We were at work…and I thought the place might be bugged."

Aran laughed softly. "Okay…well, we're home now. Let's come up with something."

"I liked your off-the-cuff explanation about a long-distance relationship. And how we dated in residency."

"Well, we knew each other then, and we did work all those awful shifts together," he stated.

"I know. It was perfect."

"Yeah, but now they'll ask us things like what side of the bed do you sleep on? Where did you honeymoon? How many windows in your bedroom?"

Ruby rubbed her eyes. "Wait—did you just say how many windows in the bedroom?"

Aran nodded. "I've heard that's been asked before."

"Well, I can easily answer that. My bedroom is a loft. It's all skylights."

"How many?"

"Four." She frowned. "No...wait..."

"You don't *know*?"

"I don't lie there and count my skylights." Aran rolled his eyes and headed to the stairs.

"Where are you going?" she asked.

"To see how many skylights are in your loft."

Ruby crossed her arms and waited for him to come back down.

"You were right. There's four," he said.

"See? You know...this is the most bizarre conversation ever."

"I think our conversation about sheep and what kind of drink we'd like to be was weirder," he teased.

"Right, I'd forgotten that."

"You never did answer that question."

"And I won't. It's still the weirdest question ever. What kind of *drink* would I be? *That's* weird."

He smiled—that handsome devilish smile she liked so much.

"So, besides us dating in residency, let's figure out our proposal story. Our current one is just me offering to enter into this marriage—it's not really great. How did I do it?"

Ruby could feel her blood heat. She didn't really want to talk about this with him. It came dangerously close to the territory they'd found themselves in when they were in Whitehead. When he'd suggested they kiss.

Just thinking about that kiss made her body thrum with excitement. She was trying to forget about that kiss, but she couldn't.

The sooner she got her Green Card the better.

Really?

"I think you got down on one knee," she said quickly, and walked over to the cupboard to make herself a cup of the decaffeinated tea that always relaxed her and put her to sleep.

She set down a mug and filled up her electric kettle.

"That's it?"

"Why does it have to be elaborate?" she asked.

"What if they ask specific questions? Like where I did it?"

"By a lake," she said quickly.

"What lake?"

Ideally she would have loved to have been down by the shores of Great Slave Lake, or beside the McKenzie River, where you could see the Deh Cho Bridge. She loved being by water, which was why she bought this house.

"My lake. I bought this house before I married you. Maybe we were out on a walk and talking about your deployment and you got down on one knee and asked me."

His expression softened. "See—was that so hard?"

"Yeah, it was."

"What do you mean?"

"I don't *do* this," she said quickly. "Relationships are not my thing. I'm not good with relationships. I never wanted to get married. The only thing I ever wanted was my career. That's it."

"I feel the same way," Aran said. "I didn't want to get married either. But marrying you was a convenience for both of us. It gave me an excuse not to get involved with anyone and it gave you a chance to get a Green Card. For better or for worse we're in this together, and we need to convince that agent that we married for love."

"How many relationships have you had?" she asked as her teapot whistled and she flicked it off.

A strange expression crossed his face. "What do you mean?"

"How many girlfriends have you had in the past?"

"A couple—but once they knew I never wanted anything serious they left. And that was fine by me. What about you? Did you leave behind someone in Canada?"

"Not really. It was the same thing. I just wanted casual and had no real time to date.

A lot of men didn't like it when I took the initiative. They didn't like me being in control." They also hadn't liked how emotionally unavailable she was.

He smiled, and his eyes twinkled as he moved closer. "I don't mind that you have control."

Her pulse began to race and she knew that she was blushing again. Every part of her was crying out to kiss him. To give in to what he was making her feel. But she couldn't. This marriage of convenience was nothing more than a business arrangement when she came right down to it—and she never mixed business with pleasure.

Even if she wanted to.

But it had been so long since she'd been with someone. Since she'd had human contact...

"It's late. I think I'm going to drink my herbal tea and just read in bed for a bit."

He nodded and rubbed the back of his neck. "Right. That's a very good plan."

"I'll see you in the morning?"

Aran nodded and headed to his room. "Yes. Have a good night, Ruby."

"You too."

She went up the stairs and heard his door shut. She let out the breath she realized she'd been holding and tried to calm her nerves.

What was it about him that made her run so hot and cold? She felt as if she was losing all control around him. Being around him made her do things and say things she'd never thought she would say or do.

And she should've known. The moment he'd walked into the hospital and introduced himself to her during their first shift together she should've realized that he was nothing but trouble.

And trouble was exactly what she didn't need.

She only *wanted* it.

CHAPTER NINE

ARAN GOT UP early and went outside to chop
some wood. It had been cold in the night and
there was no wood by the fireplace because
they'd been trapped in Whitehead. It was still
kind of damp and drizzly, but he didn't mind
going out and chopping some wood.

Besides, he couldn't sleep anyways.

All he could think about was Ruby.

That kiss that they'd shared in Whitehead
just kept playing over and over in his mind.
He'd kissed other women, but somehow
that simple kiss had stuck with him. And he
wanted to do more than just kiss her.

*You don't want a relationship and neither
does she. What could it hurt?*

And it was true. Ruby had told him herself that she didn't want anything serious beyond their sham of a marriage. She was only

legally bound to him because she wanted a Green Card.

That was it.

He knew that she was attracted to him, and he was attracted to her. *What could it hurt?* The thing was, he knew that if he indulged then someone was going to be hurt by this and he didn't want that to happen.

Aran had seen what had happened to his father when his parents had divorced. It had nearly broken him to leave his wife behind in Alaska. Aran's mother had always told him that she'd married his father out of lust, that they'd rushed into it and hadn't really talked about what they wanted, but that was not how his father viewed it.

Aran's father had loved Jessica.

Sure, he'd found love again, with Aran's stepmother, but he'd been broken for so long, pining after Jessica.

Aran never wanted that. He never wanted to feel that way and he certainly didn't want anyone to feel that way over him.

He liked Ruby. She had a bit of a tough exterior, but she really cared for people. She wanted to help people and give them everything she could. She was dedicating her life to them, flying out and rescuing people from natural disasters and accidents. Or flying to remote communities and doing a job that no other doctor or surgeon wanted to fill, because no one really wanted to live out in the middle of nowhere in one of the world's harshest climates.

Aran admired her for that.

He wished that he could stay on after they were divorced, but once this whole thing was over with he was going to return south and try to get a job somewhere. Anywhere. As soon as he got his PTSD under control.

He almost had it under control.

Who are you kidding?

He brought down the ax in one swift movement, splitting the log in two. It felt good to swing the ax—it helped him forget how he'd jumped at Ruby when she'd woken him in the clinic. For a brief moment he'd been back on the front line, lying on a stretcher after having being found in the wreckage after the IED explosion.

He could still feel the pain in his leg. The agony. And his leg gave a twinge when he thought about it. He wished that he hadn't been pieced together the way he had been. He wished that they had just taken his leg.

Then he remembered Ruby's gentle touch. Her delicate hands on his leg, working the muscles, and how good it had felt. How she made him forget about the pain. How she'd made him forget about the horrors of the front.

He winced as he picked up the logs from where they'd fallen and started a little pile.

"It'll take you all day, doing it like that."

He looked up to see Ruby leaning against the open back door in flannel pajamas, holding a cup of coffee. The steam was rising out of the top and melting away in the damp mist that clung to the trees surrounding her cabin.

"I don't like leaving a mess," he joked, and then he picked up another log.

He was trying not to look at her in her pajamas. He had never realized how sexy plaid flannel pajamas could be.

Get a grip.

Except he couldn't shake that image of her touching him. Touching the most vulnerable part of him, easing his pain with her gentleness. And how he'd wanted to reach down and kiss her, to bring her as much pleasure as she'd brought him.

He wanted to taste her lips again. He wanted to get lost in her arms.

He wanted to bare everything to her.

"I hope I didn't wake you with the wood-chopping?" he asked, trying not to think about what was under those pajamas and how much he wanted to find out.

"No, I was up," she said. "I did wonder who was chopping my wood. Why *are* you chopping my wood?"

"It was cold in the night and I couldn't sleep."

"Nightmares?"

A shiver ran down his spine and he hesitated. "Why would you say that?"

"I heard you," she said gently.

"Sorry." He felt bad that he'd woken her.

"Is it PTSD?"

"No," he snapped.

"Come on—I can see you're still suffering with the after-effects of what happened to you. You don't need to hide your post traumatic stress from me."

He didn't say anything. He didn't like her talking about it. He didn't want to talk about it with her. He didn't want to let her in. But the thing was the more he was around her the more she just wiggled her way in.

And you want to know what she's hiding from you.

"You going to pick up Chinook this morning? I kind of miss him." He was changing the subject and he didn't care. He only hoped that she didn't keep pressing him on the matter.

"No. Sam is going to keep him for a couple more days." She took a seat on the step and took a sip of her coffee. "I got a message in from Dr. Franklin. There's a typhoon blowing in and threatening the Aleutian Islands. It's wreaking havoc in the Bering Sea."

"Typhoon?"

"They're rare, but they *can* happen in southeast Alaska. Dr. Franklin wants to have a meeting and get a plan in place to fly in extra supplies and make sure we're here and ready to help the people who live along those islands."

"Will your entire team fit in your plane?" he asked.

"No, Dr. Franklin will fly another plane and I'll load up mine. We can fly together. Dr. Franklin is from Unalaska, which is part of the Aleutian Islands. He wants to make sure that everyone is taken care of there. He'll be heading out right away—we'll follow."

"Okay. Sounds good."

Aran finished his wood-chopping while Ruby sat and watched.

"That's a couple of storms and a typhoon since I started here. Maybe it's a sign," he said.

"A sign of what?" she asked.

"That I should leave Alaska," he teased.

Only he wasn't really teasing. It was best that he leave.

Sure. Run away again.

Ruby smiled. "No, it's common for early summer. The winter is worse for the islands, when the Aleutian low pressure sits there. We have a lot of bodies of water converging and meeting up. The Beaufort Sea, Bering Sea, Gulf of Alaska and the Pacific. And then you add in mountains and permafrost… Yeah, it can be a bit unpredictable."

"Just a bit!"

Ruby stood. "Keeps it interesting, though. There's coffee in the house when you're ready."

Aran nodded and watched her make her way inside. Watched her walk away. Her hair was down and loose and she looked totally relaxed and comfortable. She was *comfortable* around him. When had that happened?

And then he realized that he was at ease around her too—for the most part. He wasn't at ease when he thought about the taste of her lips or how she'd felt pressed up against him.

He finished with the last log and then set the ax into the wood block. He scooped up all the pieces he'd chopped and carried them inside.

Ruby was puttering around in the kitchen and listening to Queen. A smile tugged at the corner of his lips as he watched her dance. She was so sexy. Everything about her made him want her more. No other woman had ever gotten to him like this.

All that worry he'd been feeling fizzled away as he watched her.

She spun around and crimson bloomed in her cheeks when she saw him standing there, watching her.

"Queen?" he said quizzically as she pulled down a frying pan.

"Yeah, it's Queen. You don't like Queen?" she asked, ignoring the fact that he'd caught her awkward dancing.

"Sure—I just never would've pegged you for a fan."

"And what's a Queen fan supposed to look like?" she teased.

"You've got me. I don't know. I just never would have thought you were one."

"I *love* the immortal Freddie. Plus, I like listening to them when I cook."

"What're you cooking?" he asked.

"Scrambled eggs. Want some?"

"Sure."

Aran slowly knelt down. He was a bit stiff, but he managed to hide the pain he was feeling from Ruby because she was distracted by making breakfast. He stacked the logs neatly.

"Well, at least I now know what you wear to bed and that you listen to Queen while you cook."

She glanced over her shoulder as she cracked eggs into the frying pan. "And what music do *you* like?"

"Country."

"I like that too."

"You're an eclectic music listener, are you?"

"Yeah, I like what I like and it's all over the board. But I only listen to certain music at certain times. Like rock or metal while I cook—but metal from the seventies. And when I drive it's usually The Hip."

"Yeah... I'm just a country fan. I don't mind Queen, though."

"Good, because I'm not turning it off."

She finished scrambling the eggs while Aran washed his hands and sat down at the kitchen island. She dished out a plate of scrambled eggs and he poured himself a cup of coffee.

"Thanks," he said as he sat down to eat his eggs.

"Thanks for the morning wood."

He almost choked on his eggs. *"What?"*

She flushed pink and groaned. "Oh, Creator! That's not what I meant at all."

He chuckled. "That's okay. I understand what you meant and it was no problem."

"We have *got* to get over this awkwardness. I mean, we're friends, right?"

"Yeah, sure."

Only he didn't think of her as a friend. And he really didn't *want* to think of her as a friend. He wanted to think of her as more than that, only he couldn't let himself. It wasn't fair to her. There was nothing he could give her.

"I'm going to get ready for the day. I want to get to the hospital and help Dr. Franklin plan before he gets agitated that I'm not there."

"Sounds good. I'll be waiting."

Aran watched her disappear up the stairs and finished his breakfast in silence. He had to pull himself together. They could be friends and they could work together. Nothing more.

There couldn't be anything more between them.

She was kicking herself for saying that.

Thanks for the morning wood? How could you be so silly?

It had taken her off-guard to wake up to the sound of wood being cut, and when she'd gone downstairs to see a shirtless Aran cutting up firewood it had made her think about a lot of inappropriate things.

He might have an injury, but he was still a strong man. A capable man. Not the man she'd thought he was when they'd first met. The arrogant playboy who'd got on her nerves but whom she'd never been able to shake. This man—he belonged here. It was as if he fit right in with her life and that thought scared her. There was no room in her life for anyone but herself and Chinook.

Oh, really?

She jumped into the shower and heard the ax again. She looked out the small window and watched him out there again as the water ran over her. Her blood heated and she turned the cold water on, hoping it would clear her head of all the naughty thoughts of Aran running through her mind.

Thoughts of him scooping her up in his arms and carrying her to the bed...of herself running her hands over his chest and tasting his kisses again.

She cranked the cold water up some more, hoping it would work.

It didn't.

"Dr. Franklin, you're taking the team and getting set up in Unalaska. Dr. Atkinson and I will bring the rest of the supplies and meet you there by the end of the day." Ruby went down her check list for the meeting. "Do you have your flight plan?"

"Yes." Dr. Franklin pulled out the printout of the plan he had submitted.

Ruby looked it over. "Going a little bit out of the way?"

"The weather system is bringing a low, which is strange for this time of year. I want to avoid it if at all possible. I flew planes through the Aleutian Islands long before I became a doctor," said Dr. Franklin. "I want to get there and set up in the emergency shelter before the storm hits."

"Okay—well, you have your team. You're taking John and Lindsey. I'll file a flight plan to join you later. When you arrive tell me what you need and I'll bring it along with me."

Dr. Franklin nodded. "Sure thing, Dr. Cloutier."

"Okay, let's get this done, then."

Franklin, John and Lindsey got up to start work. Ruby had to stay behind and finish her rotation on the trauma floor. They would arrive before the storm made landfall.

Aran had sat quietly in the meeting not saying much. He looked a little tired and she wasn't surprised, since he'd told her that he hadn't slept much the night before. Not that she'd slept much either, knowing he was having nightmares, and she couldn't stop thinking about this morning, with him at the wood pile.

Once the others had left her office she sat down on the edge of her desk. "You okay?"

"What?" he asked, as if he had been zoning out.

"You look like you're ready to fall asleep."

"Yeah, I feel like I *could* sleep." He scrubbed his hand over his face.

"Why don't you have a rest in the on-call room? I need you with your wits about you when we head to Unalaska."

Aran pursed his lips together, much as his mother did when she was about to deliver bad news or when she was unhappy or worried. "I don't know if I should go."

"What do you mean?" Ruby asked, confused.

"A typhoon? Getting stuck somewhere with you for a couple of days?" Aran said. "We haven't talked about the kiss since it happened and I don't like this awkwardness."

A blush crept up her neck. "It won't be like Whitehead, Aran. Franklin, John and Lindsey will all be there. And Unalaska is bigger than Whitehead—there are other small communities surrounding it and people will be coming to the storm shelter. I need you up there. I need all hands on deck."

"Well, if that's the case…"

"It'll be fine. We're not going to do that again. We're not going to…"

She couldn't even bring herself to say it—because she *wanted* to kiss him again. Even though she knew it was a bad idea, she still wanted it.

She wanted more from him.

She might not have had a lot of relationships, or anything meaningful, but he was the first man she really desired. The first man who had stirred something deep down inside her.

Still, she couldn't let herself give in to temptation. She'd promised herself that. The kiss had been a one-time thing. It had been done in order to break the tension between them and that was it.

"We could be doing medical procedures. It won't be—"

"Yeah," he said cutting her off. "You're right. We have to stop being so awkward around each other."

"Exactly."

They had been doing fine until that kiss. Perhaps this was karma's way of paying her back for this deceitful marriage?

"So what do you need me to do?" he asked.

She handed him a sheet. "Get the medical supplies ready. I'm doing a first round of those patients who are still in the emergency room. Then the surgical patients and then I'm free."

Aran nodded. "I'll get these ready for you."

"Meet me down in the ambulance pod in three hours. An ambulance will take us and the supplies to the airport in no time. I'm going to file a flight plan now and then do my rounds."

"All right. I'll see you then."

Aran left the office, and once he did she was finally able to relax a bit after thinking about him and her in Whitehead.

She had to get better control over herself. She wasn't doing a very good job.

When she'd woken up that morning to Dr. Franklin's email, she had not expected to find Aran outside chopping wood. She had watched him from the kitchen while her coffee had been brewing.

She'd been completely mesmerized by the way he moved. How easily he had split the wood. How Alaska seemed to suit him, even if he *did* insist that he much preferred the south. It was as if he belonged with her.

And all she'd been able to think about was how he'd made her feel. How she'd wanted to continue that kiss. How she'd wanted to lose control over him.

She hated the way he affected her so much.

Maybe you should've sent him with Dr. Franklin?

The problem was that Dr. Franklin didn't completely trust Aran. None of the team did. It was better that Aran came with her. He was still on probation.

Ruby had no doubt that after this mission the other team members would see what a valuable asset he was to the team and then they would all feel comfortable working with him. They would trust him.

In order to make a team like hers work there had to be a high level of trust. If there was no trust then it was doomed to fail from the start.

The team had to believe there was complete trust between her and Aran—which there was. But Aran and her were married. Married couples were intimate, not awkward around each other. At least all the married couples she knew…

Aran did exactly what was needed and got all the supplies. Ruby's rounds took longer because an accident came in. Someone had collided with a moose on the highway and she was called in to emergency surgery.

When she got out she saw Dr. Franklin had landed in Unalaska and had forwarded a list of supplies he needed. It was a lot more than they'd thought. Apparently the last shipment of the most vital medical supplies hadn't come in on time. So she spent an hour trying to collect everything from the list that she could, so they could prepare for the typhoon when it made landfall.

Aran was loading up the rig when she arrived.

"You're late," he said.

"Emergency trauma came in. Someone hit a moose on the highway. And then Dr. Franklin sent his list and it turns out that Unalaska needs some more supplies." She lifted one of the kits into the back of the rig. "I then had to adjust our departure time because we're leaving later. I just hope the weather holds."

"Me too."

They finished loading and then got into the back. The ambulance driver raced them to the airport with the sirens blaring. Ruby was glad of that, because right now it was a race to get to Unalaska before the typhoon hit.

Her plane was ready and waiting and Aran and the ambulance driver helped her load up. She could see dark clouds far across the horizon. Anchorage was supposed to get the tail end of the storm. It would be heavy rainfall and some wind, but nothing compared to Unalaska and the rest of the most westerly tip of the Aleutian Islands. When the Bering Sea became stormy it became a dangerous place.

Once the plane was loaded she prepared for take-off and was given clearance right away, because her flight was considered an emergency. It was a smooth takeoff, but it wasn't long before she realized that they hadn't beaten the storm and she was flying straight into it. The turbulence became wicked.

"I think we'll have to turn back," she shouted into her microphone.

"I think you're right," Aran responded.

He looked a little pale as the wind jostled

the plane around. He was nervous and she couldn't blame him—she was nervous too.

She made her course correction and had just started to turn and head back to Anchorage when the engine light came on.

Oh, Creator. No.

"What's wrong?" Aran asked when he noticed the flashing lights and alarms.

"I lost an engine. I'm going to have to make an emergency landing. There's an old town not far from here that has an old airstrip."

"What do you mean, an old town?" he asked, and she could hear the panic in his voice.

"No one lives there anymore, but there are buildings and a runway. It's used in emergency situations like this. It'll be okay," she reassured him. "We're fine. We're just going to land. Hang on."

After a few tense moments Ruby caught sight of the airfield that was always maintained. The town was an old ghost town, but often bush pilots that had been chartered by hunting outfits used this airstrip to drop off guides who would take parties into the wilderness to hunt. Especially in the summer.

She turned her plane sideways and made a tight crab landing on the gravel strip that ran alongside a riverbank. Her plane sputtered as she made the landing and then came to a halt, with the other engine giving up and starting to smoke.

Ruby breathed a sigh of relief—and then cursed under her breath as she climbed out of the plane and went to look at the engine. She could see a leak and she cursed again.

The wind was strong and howling down off the mountains into the little valley where they had landed. She could see the storm clouds moving in fast. They were close to the Aleutian Islands and right in the path of the edge of the storm. It wasn't raining yet, but the temperature was dropping with the low pressure moving in.

It wasn't the rain that bothered Ruby at the moment, but the wind speed.

"What're we going to do?" Aran shouted over the wind.

"We'll cover my plane and then seek shelter in the old airport. It's an emergency shelter and it's kept stocked. We'll have to wait out this storm and then radio for help. With a leak in one of the engines I can't get this plane off the ground."

"And what about Dr. Franklin?" Aran asked.

Ruby sighed. "He knows what to do. We'll get this plane fixed and then we can help with the clean-up after. As much as I hate this, there's nothing else to do."

She pulled out a tarp from the back of her plane and began to lash the covering down. The last thing she needed was the storm doing even more damage. After she'd finished securing it she jammed blocks under the wheels and hoped to heck that the plane would withstand the winds that were now whipping down through this wind tunnel of a ghost town.

When she was done the rain came down in a sheet, soaking them instantly. They ran for the shelter of the metal U-shaped airport. There was an old transistor radio for emergencies, but best of all there was a wood stove in the center of the room.

With the temperature dropping the rain had felt like knives cutting at her skin. Her teeth were chattering as she helped Aran collect wood from the lean-to attached to the entrance so they could start a fire.

It wasn't long before they had a nice fire going, but they were still so soaking wet there was no way they were ever going to warm up.

She knew that they had to get out of their clothes.

Aran was already peeling off his wet clothing and hanging it on the line that ran across the room. He glanced at her, shivering. She knew she needed to get out of her own clothes, but she didn't want to do that in front of him.

"I'll get it."

He went to the storage locker and brought back some Army blankets. He strung them up, making a room divider, and stepped onto the colder side, leaving her by the stove.

"Get undressed and wrap a blanket around

you. It's not ideal, but you really don't want to catch pneumonia, now, do you?"

"No," she said through her chattering teeth.

She quickly began to peel off her clothes and hung them on the line. The rain pelted like hammers against the metal roof while the wind howled like a banshee. It made her shiver even more, listening to it.

In all her years in Alaska she had never been in a typhoon before. They were rare. They never got typhoons in the Northwest Territories. The worst storm she'd ever been in had been a bad thunderstorm in Southern Ontario when she was going there to university, but that had been nothing compared to this.

And it was amplified by the fact that she was stuck in a small room, powerless to help her team and getting naked in front of her fake husband.

She knew one thing. It was going to be a very long night.

CHAPTER TEN

RUBY WAS HUDDLED on the floor and trying to keep warm. The wood stove was great, and did the job of heating the whole small space they were sharing, but it was nothing like a good crackling fire.

The makeshift wall parted and she saw that Aran had a blanket wrapped around him. He sat down close to her, next to the wood stove. The wind was howling outside and the rain was lashing the side of the building hard. Ruby trembled again.

"Did you take off everything?" Aran asked.

"Yes, but I can't seem to get warm." She pulled the blanket around her tighter.

Aran scooted closer and leaned against her, trying to give her some of his body heat. She was nervous about how close he was, knowing that the only thing between them was a couple of blankets.

Thinking about that made her tremble—not from the cold, but from something else.

Even though she shouldn't, she leaned her head against him. It felt nice. It made her feel safe, even though she was afraid about what might happen if she just let him in. If she gave in to all the strange emotions that he stirred in her.

No one had ever affected her this way. Aran made her feel alive. She wanted him, desired him, and she cared about him.

She'd never cared about someone this much.

She'd never *wanted* to care about someone like this—especially after she'd watched her mother grieve over her father for years. Her mother never had got over Papa.

Ruby let out a long sigh. The thought of caring about someone so much, loving someone so much and losing them, was unbearable.

On those days when she lost the battle with death and lost a patient she'd see the pain in the family's faces and know what they were feeling. She knew that pain, and she didn't ever want to experience that kind of trauma again. It was too hard. It was too much.

But being around Aran stirred up feelings that she'd never thought she'd have and it was scary how much he affected her.

"What're you thinking about?" Aran asked gently.

"What?" she asked.

"You let out a sigh."

"I was thinking of my father. I was thinking about when he died."

"Tell me about that," he said softly.

She didn't want to. She'd never talked about it with anyone before and she was terrified. But a little voice urged her to tell him. To let it out. To free herself from the burden she had carried around for so long. Alone.

"He was killed working in a diamond mine where there were no roads. There were no medical staff at the mine—which was a huge no-no. There was a winter storm that slowed getting help up there, and by the time the air ambulance got to him he was gone. If he'd have had the same injury in a city, or if medical staff had been there, he would've lived."

"I'm sorry to hear that. It explains why you're so dedicated to your job. That's admirable."

"Thank you." Tears welled up in her eyes as she thought about her father. "I never talk about him with anyone."

"Thanks for talking about it with me."

She nodded. "I saw the pain my mother went through, losing him. They were best friends. You know, they both went to the same residential school and they just formed a bond there. To survive. They lost track of each other when the last of those schools was shut down and they were sent back to their parents. My mother came from a reserve in northern Alberta and my dad was Bechokǫ̀ but they met up again when they were given the chance to go to college. My parents both wanted to better themselves, and to forget about residential school and everything they'd lost. Anyways, long story short, they got married and had kids. Papa taught me so much and then... I watched my mother grieve him and I just... I couldn't ever..." Tears slipped down her cheek. "It's not easy for me to let someone in."

Aran nodded. "I understand. I watched my parents go through divorce and I watched my dad grieve. My mother wasn't dead, but it was a different kind of loss. I knew I never wanted to go through that. I have no interest in that kind of pain. Of course, who does?"

"No one does."

He nodded. "And I'm still not whole. Not whole after what happened to me at the front line. I'm not going to tie someone down. I'm not going to make someone else suffer because of what I do."

"I understand. Probably more than most."

He nodded. "Yeah. I know you do."

She smiled and Aran leaned in and wiped the tears from her cheek with his thumb. The simple touch made her body tremble with delight and she reached out and touched him. "I'm glad you're here with me."

"I'm glad I'm here too."

And before she could stop herself, before

she let the controlled and rational side of her take over, she kissed him.

The blanket slipped down off her shoulders as Aran kissed her back, his fingers moving to her hair. She moved closer. She knew she shouldn't reach out and kiss Aran again, but she couldn't help herself.

Right now she wanted to lose control. She wanted to *feel*. She wanted this. She chose this. She couldn't fight it anymore. She wanted Aran as she had never wanted another man.

It was overpowering. Primal.

It thrilled her.

Made her feel alive.

How long had she been so numb? She didn't know. All she knew was that Aran made her feel something she'd never felt before, and even though it scared her she couldn't stop.

"Ruby," he whispered against her hair. "Are you sure? I can't promise you anything beyond what we have now."

"Yes. I'm sure. And you know I can't promise you anything either, but I *want* this, Aran."

"I want this too. I have since the first time

I met you and you looked me up and down with such indifference."

"I was your challenge," she teased. "Sorry."

"No, you were more than that. It wasn't that. You were strong and I admired it. Never be sorry for that, or for who you are."

Ruby pulled him down to the floor and Aran laid kisses on her lips, her neck and lower. His strong hands roved over her body, igniting the flames that burned in her veins.

"Ruby, you make me feel like I've never felt before."

He brushed a kiss against her lips, lightly, then deepened the kiss into an urgent need that made her body sing. They were skin to skin, pressed against each other, and it felt so right. She opened her legs to let him settle between her thighs. She arched her hips, wanting to feel all of him.

"Ruby," Aran moaned. "We have to stop."

"Why?" she asked.

"I don't have protection."

"It's okay. I'm on birth control. Don't stop. Please don't stop." She just wanted to have this moment and she didn't care about the consequences.

"Are you sure?"

"Yes. Are *you* sure?" She bucked her hips and he groaned.

"God, yes."

"How much do you want it?" she teased.

Aran kissed her again, his tongue pushing past her lips, claiming her. He ran his hands over her, driving her wild with need. Ruby pulled him closer and wrapped her legs around his waist.

"You're so beautiful. From that first moment I saw you five years ago I've wanted you," he murmured.

His hands slid between them and he began to stroke her. Ruby cried out at his touch. She wanted so much more. She wanted Aran to be inside her, to take her and claim her. She just wanted to forget everything. She wanted to forget her lonely life. Forget the storm that had forced them to land. Forget all the rules she'd put in place to protect her heart from pain—the rules that guarded her heart from feeling any kind of love.

She wanted to forget it all and have this moment with him.

"Ruby," Aran whispered. "You feel so soft. I want you."

"I want you too." She kissed him. "I've always wanted you...since I first met you."

Aran slowly entered her, filling her, and her body shuddered in pleasure. Being joined with him was exactly what she needed. What she wanted. She moved her hips, urging him to move faster, but Aran took his time and it drove her wild.

She wanted him hard and fast. Her instinct was to control him even now, to take control over the situation as she always did, but Aran was in control. It scared her, but she let all those inhibitions melt away. Aran was controlling the pace and he was taking his time and it drove her wild.

She moved in time with him. Her eyes locked with his in the dim light. The only sound was their breathing, their little cries of pleasure. The storm and everything else that weighed them down were miles away.

All she had in this moment was him.

It was just the two of them.

"Come for me…" He whispered the command. "Come for me, Ruby."

"I don't want this to end."

She arched her body to press herself against him, tighter, and he trailed kisses down her neck, his hands cupping her breast.

"Come for me," he repeated. "Let it go."

And as she let him control the moment she could feel her body succumbing to the sweet release she was searching for. The release she so desperately needed and wanted.

It was unlike anything she'd ever felt before. Her body tingled as pleasure overtook her and she cried out, digging her nails into his back as she came around him. She wanted to hold on to this moment. Never to let go.

As her body drifted down from her release his rhythm picked up and he thrust hard and fast, seeking his own. She moved her hips, wanting him to come. Now she had some control over him, urging him on, and with the subtle movements of her hips it wasn't long until his own release came.

Aran rolled away and she curled up against him. He put his arm around her, holding her close, and then pulled a blanket over them as they lay on the floor next to the wood stove. She laid her head on his chest and listened to the reassuring sound of his heart.

They said nothing. There was nothing to say. No promises had been made and she didn't want them. Or she thought she didn't. This had been about human contact. That was it.

Really?

She shook the thought away. She wouldn't allow it in. She didn't want to feel anything more than what they had shared here, this night. Their marriage wasn't real and it had a time limit. Tonight had been about human contact, warmth and comfort. Just two lonely and broken souls reaching out to one another.

That was it.

She knew that, but there was a part of her that wanted more. A part of her that had never been here before. A part of her that wanted just a fraction of what her mother and father had had—which scared her.

It was the part of her that wanted love.

That wanted happiness.

That wanted more than just convenience.

Aran listened to the even, steady breaths of Ruby as she slept. He liked that she was curled up against him.

He had risked all his self-control, every part of him, when he had moved to the other side of the curtain.

He had rationalized it by telling himself he was just trying to survive. He was just trying to keep her warm. That was all. They were both cold and the last thing they needed was hypothermia while they waited for help out in the middle of nowhere.

She had looked so beautiful, sitting there. Her soft, silken hair curling as the heat from the wood stove dried it. Her body glowing in the light. And then she'd reached over and kissed him.

The moment she'd kissed him he'd been a lost man. His body had burned with need and he'd wanted her. He'd wanted her for a long time.

It had thrilled him that she'd wanted him too, though he'd been nervous. He'd wanted to be with her, but he hadn't wanted to hurt her. All he could give her was this night. He wouldn't burden her with his pain, with his hurt, with his ghosts.

Being with her and having nothing between them was more dangerous than being out in that storm.

So he had been nervous, but he hadn't been able to pull himself away when she'd told him she wanted him just as much as he wanted her. Her hands on his skin had made him feel as if he was on fire. Her lips on his had made him ache with need.

He'd forgotten what a woman's touch felt like.

He'd forgotten what passion tasted like.

He wasn't even sure that what he'd had before had ever been like this. He couldn't recall ever wanting a woman so much that it had taken every ounce of his control not to rush through it.

It had never burned so slow as it had with Ruby.

What he'd shared with her tonight had been something completely different. He had been completely lost to her.

And, God help him, he wanted more.

Only he couldn't have more.

He wouldn't put his heart at risk—especially with someone who didn't want commitment either.

Love just brought pain.

Who said anything about love?

The thought caught him off-guard. He shouldn't have given in to Ruby. He should have held back when she'd kissed him.

But when it came to Ruby and her heady kisses he was a lost man. He couldn't help himself. So he wanted more. But it just wasn't meant to be.

Even if it could never happen again he would

always care for her. He would always cherish this shared night together.

His heart was guarded, just as much as hers was, but it had been wonderful even just for a moment to share something so deep and intimate with her. To have that connection with someone.

It saddened him that it had just been a brief moment, and it frightened him that it didn't feel like enough. Deep down, he knew that if he didn't put some distance between him and Ruby he would never be able to let her go.

He knew he would always want more.

CHAPTER ELEVEN

THE SOUND OF the radio crackling woke him up and he shivered, realizing that the fire in the wood stove had gone out. There was silence except for the sound of Ruby beside him, sleeping still.

Aran got up and peered out the small window in the radio room. The storm was over. There were a few downed trees, and it was still raining, but not heavily. The runway, at least, was clear of trees.

He padded back into the other room and found his clothes were dry. He slipped them on.

Ruby stirred then. "What's going on?" she asked drowsily.

"The storm's over and the radio is back on."

"The radio is on?" She sat up and wrapped a

blanket around herself, running into the other room to call for assistance.

After Aran was dressed he grabbed some more wood from the woodpile. Thankfully there were a few embers that were still burning and it wouldn't take much to get a full fire going again. He knew how to do that.

Ruby came back into the room. "I got a hold of someone in Anchorage. They're sending out a mechanic to take a look at the plane and hopefully we can get airborne again and fly to Unalaska."

"Were you able to contact anyone there?"

She shook her head. "No, but I know that they've been looking for us since we didn't arrive. Anchorage was very glad to hear my call signal."

He nodded. "Good. I'm sorry I let the fire die out. Are you cold?"

"A bit—but are the clothes dry?" she asked. "Yeah."

"I'll just get dressed."

Ruby slipped past him and went behind the curtain to get dressed. He tried not to think about her, naked behind that curtain, but try as he might images of her in his arms last night flashed through his mind.

He closed the door to the wood stove and then moved to the cabinet, where he hoped there would be some canned food. He opened the door and was met with nothing.

"Rats," he mumbled.

"What?" Ruby asked, pulling down the curtain now that she was dressed.

"I was hoping for some food."

"Check the gear bag I brought in last night. There's some freeze-dried survival food in there. It's not the best, but you won't starve eating that."

"I know. I've lived on it before."

He picked up her gear bag and set it on the worktop. He found the stash of freeze-dried food. All they needed was to add some water.

Ruby found the kettle that went on the stove. She filled it with water and set it on top.

"What would you like for breakfast?" Aran asked as he went through the selection—which wasn't much. He kept digging and then pulled out a bag. "How about a breakfast skillet? Hash browns and scrambled eggs mixed with sausage?"

"Sounds good. At least that's a breakfast type of food. There should be instant coffee in there too."

Aran dug down further and found it. "We're all set."

"I like to be prepared. It's the Girl Guide in me."

"Is that like a Girl Scout?" Aran asked.

"Yep."

Ruby used a towel and picked the kettle off the top of the stove. Aran divided up the freeze-dried contents and added water to rehydrate it. It didn't look appetizing, but Aran was pretty sure he'd eaten worse. And the coffee might be instant but, again, he wasn't going to look a gift horse in the mouth.

"Well, I guess if one of the questions is how we spent our honeymoon…"

Ruby blushed and then laughed. "Yeah, I suppose you're right. Jeez, you could've picked a nicer place."

Aran smiled, and was relieved that she was joking. Maybe this would be okay. Maybe this would work even if he wanted to be more than friends.

But he couldn't promise her anything. He couldn't promise her forever.

Why not?

"I hope Dr. Franklin and his team managed okay," Aran said, changing the subject so that he wouldn't have to think about it.

"I hope so too. And I hope the typhoon wasn't as strong as they were predicting and that it just dissipated over the islands and into the Bering Sea. They're so rare here, and usually by the time they reach Alaska they've lost steam."

"Roger, bush camp base. Can you hear me?" The radio crackled.

Ruby got up and ran into the radio room. "Roger that, BX7935. We can hear you loud and clear."

"Bush camp base, I've got a fix on your location and I'm just circling to make a safe landing. See you short."

"Roger." Ruby craned her neck to look out the window.

Aran could hear the plane coming in. Hopefully it wouldn't take too long to fix up the plane and they could get out of here and back to work.

He knew that Ruby was anxious to find out what had happened to Dr. Franklin and the others in Unalaska. And Aran was anxious to put some distance between them and this cabin where they'd been alone.

He needed to throw himself back into work and get his mindset back on track. Then he could put what had happened behind him. They could move forward, as the plan had always been.

Who are you kidding?

"You're all fixed, Dr. Cloutier," said Stewart, the mechanic. "You're lucky that you were able to land safely. I'm glad this didn't happen out over the water when the storm was at its worst."

"Me too, Stewart. I'm still annoyed that it

happened at all. There's supplies I needed to get out to Unalaska. Do you know how they fared?"

"Typhoon was pretty strong when it made landfall on the leeward side of the island. I'm hoping it just blew over, but I know they lost power and communications for a while. I can tell you that Seward Memorial was quite worried about you two when your plane didn't check in and Unalaska reported you missing."

"It was a bad situation all around." Ruby finished going over the plane. "I appreciate it, Stewart. I owe you a drink for coming out here and fixing my plane."

"Sounds like a plan. Come on, Rick. We have to get back to Anchorage."

Rick, the pilot of the other plane, nodded to Stewart and shook Aran's hand. Ruby walked back to where Aran was standing and they waited until Stewart and Rick's plane had taken off toward Anchorage.

"You ready?" Ruby asked.

"More than ready."

Ruby grabbed the gear she'd brought inside

and Aran made sure the fire in the wood stove was out and that everything was back the way it should be, just in case someone else needed a place to stay in an emergency.

They loaded the gear into the back of the plane and Ruby took her place in the cockpit. She was glad to get back into the sky. It was still drizzly and gray out, with the after-effects of the typhoon that had blown in, but it was nothing like yesterday. And at least there was no fog.

She just hoped that she'd have a clear place to land in Unalaska. But Unalaska Airport—or Dutch Harbor—was better than this one, and they would have lights and an air traffic controller.

She just hoped that Dr. Franklin, John and Lindsey had managed to fare well without them…

It was just a short plane ride from where they'd spent the night to Unalaska.

"That's the Bering Sea, over there," Ruby pointed out.

"Not far from Russia, then?"

"Nope." Ruby smiled. "I'm glad the weather is cooperating, but the sea is a little choppy."

"I don't aim to go swimming," Aran joked.

"Me neither."

As they approached the airport Ruby made contact with the air traffic controller and was given clearance to land. It was a little windy, but she was able to bring the plane down gently and taxi to the location where she'd been told to park.

When she got out of the plane Dr. Franklin was waiting with a truck.

"Thank God you two are okay," he said as he came up to them.

Aran opened the hatch and helped to offload the supplies.

"Yeah, I lost an engine and I was forced to land at that old abandoned airstrip that serves as a bush camp starting point. You know the one?" Ruby said.

Dr. Franklin nodded. "Good. I'm so glad. The supplies are needed. There were some injuries when the typhoon hit, but nothing serious. The town fared well, but we're still out of power. We're mostly camped out in the town's recreation center. There were also some strong storm surges and there's quite a bit of damage from that. We could use your help, though. John was trying to help some civilians and he dislocated his shoulder."

"Ouch. Did you reset it?"

Franklin nodded. "I was able to get an X-ray before the back-up generator was damaged by a storm surge. He's on some strong pain-killers, so it's been just me and Lindsey running the show all night. We're waiting for the National Guard to get in and help restore power."

"Well, Dr. Atkinson and I are here now."

And apparently they were there in the nick of time. She could see that Dr. Franklin was exhausted, and she was worried about John. He would be out of action for some time.

They finished loading the supplies into the truck Franklin had borrowed and then climbed in and headed toward the recreation center.

There were downed trees and flooding near

the water. Ships in the harbor had been damaged and some had been capsized. Fishing and crabbing were the main industries in Unalaska and a lot of livelihoods and money would be lost.

It was a slow and bumpy ride, but it didn't take them long to navigate the debris on the road to the recreation center. Lindsey was waiting with a group of residents, who let out a cheer when Ruby climbed out of the truck.

Ruby could see Lindsey visibly relax as she came over to give Ruby a hug.

"I was so worried about you," Lindsey said. "I know you're a good pilot, but that was a wicked storm."

"I only caught the tail-end of it. I had an engine failure and had to turn back."

"Good thing you did," Lindsey said. "It's been a wild night, and with John injured it's been a hard slog for Dr. Franklin and me."

"We're here now," Aran said as he picked up one of the boxes and followed Dr. Franklin inside.

"Right," Ruby stated, and grabbed a couple

of gear bags. "We're here now, so you can get some rest. Show me what you've set up and we'll get right to work."

There weren't many really bad injuries, but more people from the smaller outlying islands were being brought in by boat.

While Dr. Franklin and Lindsey rested Ruby and Aran took over seeing all the patients. Ruby didn't have to explain anything to Aran about how she usually ran a makeshift medical clinic in the aftermath of a natural disaster. His Army training meant he knew exactly what to do.

And now she was questioning herself as to why she'd been so against him in the first place—why she'd wanted to hire and train someone herself. That would have taken time, and they wouldn't have been able to treat as many people as efficiently as they were now.

She watched him work on the other side of the gymnasium and couldn't help but smile. He was the perfect ying to her yang. They worked so well together.

You don't want love, remember? You don't want a relationship.

She tore her gaze away. What had she been thinking? Why had she given in to her needs and kissed him? She was putting her heart in jeopardy. She didn't have it in her to leave herself open to the possibility of pain. The possibility of losing someone.

Really?

The thing was, a part of her wanted to explore that with Aran. Maybe, just maybe, it would be worth the risk if she had someone like Aran by her side...

"Dr. Cloutier, there's been an accident with the crew clearing off a section of road near the mountain. There's been a rock slide and there's an injured man up on the pass."

"Your husband died from crush injuries. If we'd only got to him sooner, Mrs. Cloutier."

She could hear the doctor's voice in her head. She could hear her mother crying and it made her heart skip a beat—because that was something she didn't want to think about.

Not right now.

Not here.

"Okay," she said quickly, shaking the ghost of the memory away. "Okay."

Aran was looking at her and she could see the concern on his face. She waved him over and he came as quickly as he could.

"Is everything all right?" he asked.

"Get a trauma kit ready. Prep it for a crush injury. There's a man who has been caught in a landslide and he needs medical attention. We need to get up there as soon as possible."

"Sure."

Aran disappeared into the annex where they were keeping the supplies. Ruby collected up some other gear that they would need and then called the airport to ready a flight plan back to Anchorage.

She was not going to let this man die here.

She wasn't going to let him die like her father.

By the time they had collected everything they needed it was raining as the tail-end of the typhoon drifted through.

The crewman who had come to get her

drove Aran and her toward where the land-slide had happened.

Come on.

Every second that passed made her all the more anxious. When her father had died his life had hung in the balance for a matter of minutes, so the longer it took them in the rain the more upset she was, thinking that they weren't going to make it in time.

Don't think like that.

She couldn't let herself think like that. This was why she had developed her trauma team—this was why she'd become a surgeon. She'd left the north to head to a larger city that had been overwhelming and strange just so that she could return to the place that was home and save others.

No one had to die needlessly.

There were flares on the road, visible even through the sheets of rain that were falling.

"We're here," the crewman said. "Be care-ful, though. With this rain we're at risk of an-other landslide."

Ruby nodded and grabbed a gear bag, and

Aran followed closely behind her. The rain jacket she'd borrowed from the recreation center did nothing, really. She was still getting soaked as she followed the other members of the road crew around the rubble to where lanterns were lit and a tarp had been erected.

Ruby's heart sank when she saw the man. *No.*

She looked over at Aran and saw his jaw was clenched. He gave a slight shake of his head and pulled her aside.

"What do you think?" she asked, but she already knew the answer.

"There's nothing we can do. Look at the rocks on his body. We remove those rocks and he'll bleed out. His crush injuries are probably severe."

"Probably," Ruby snapped. "We don't know for sure."

When she looked at the man under the rubble all she could see was her father's face looking back at her and a lump formed in her throat.

Papa.

"The most we can do is make him comfortable until he passes," Aran whispered.

"I'm going to do everything I can to save him."

"Ruby, it's a lost cause," Aran said. "Even on the front lines we knew when it was time to let go."

Ruby ignored him and moved toward the man. "Gerald, I'm here."

Gerald, the man who was trapped, barely looked at her.

"Gerald? I'm Dr. Cloutier and I'm here to help."

"Oh. Okay." Gerald was shivering and looking around him.

"Can you feel anything, Gerald? Are you in any pain?" Ruby asked, kneeling next to him.

"No," Gerald responded. "No. Not in pain. Just want to get out of here. I have some errands to run."

He was delirious. Ruby glanced out of the corner of her eye to see that Aran was speaking gently to the foreman. She was angry that he was giving up hope. That was not what *she* did. She saved lives. She didn't just walk away.

"I'm glad you're not in any pain," Ruby whispered.

"Who are you?" he asked again.

"I'm Dr. Cloutier, but you can call me Ruby."

"Ruby…that's a pretty name."

"Thank you."

She set up her equipment. She had pain medication, but she wanted to save that for when they moved the boulders. She glanced up at the rubble and could see the size of the rocks that were pinning him down. Her heart sank.

His spine was most likely shattered, which was why he wasn't in any pain.

"I can't see!" Gerald called out in a panic. "I can't see."

Ruby choked back the tears that were threatening to overtake her. "It's okay, it's raining and it's pretty dark. Why don't you close your eyes and try to rest? We'll get these rocks off you in a moment."

"Okay." Gerald closed his eyes.

"There was nothing to be done, Mrs. Cloutier. His spine was crushed."

Aran came and stood close to her. "Ruby?"

"No," she whispered to him. *"No."*

Aran sank down beside her.

Gerald's breathing became labored and she watched him slip away. Hot tears slid down her cheeks as Gerald took his last breath on the side of the mountain.

"Time of death: twenty-thirty," Aran stated.

The men on Gerald's crew took off their hats and looked solemn.

"You can dig him out now," Aran said gently.

Ruby cursed and stormed off into the rain. She walked away from where everything was happening. She had to put distance between herself and that senseless, pointless death.

Tears streamed down her face and she just stared up into the rain.

"Ruby...?" Aran said.

"Leave me alone!" she snapped.

"Ruby, there was nothing—"

"Don't tell me there was nothing we could've done. We had everything to save that man. *Everything!* We're both surgeons. I could've taken him to the rec center and had him stabilized. I had my plane ready to take him to Anchorage. He should've survived. My father had *nothing*! That's why he died. That's why he died and that's why I've given my whole life to the north—to saving lives so that people like my papa and Gerald don't have to die!"

"We're not God, Ruby. We can only do so much."

"You'd given up on him before we even got to him. Admit it."

"I won't!" Aran said hotly. "But when I saw him I knew there was no saving him. Ruby, his spine was crushed. There's no way he could've survived that."

"Every minute counts. If you had been quicker…" She regretted the words as soon as they'd slipped out of her mouth.

His eyes narrowed. "If my leg hadn't slowed us down? Fine—blame me. But nothing could've saved Gerald. And probably not your father either, given the fact it sounds like he died of a crush injury as well."

Ruby slapped him. "Don't you *dare* talk about my father! You don't know anything about it. You don't know anything about *me!*"

Aran touched his face. "You're right. I don't. But this marriage isn't real and soon enough we can go our separate ways."

He turned around and left her standing in the rain, weeping.

Weeping for her father, weeping for the patients she couldn't save, weeping for all she'd given to the north and how she could never save her father's life no matter how much of her life she gave.

Her father was never coming back and she was alone.

CHAPTER TWELVE

THE FLIGHT BACK to Anchorage the next day was solemn and quiet. Lindsey had decided to fly with Ruby, and Aran had stayed behind to help with John, who was still in a lot of pain from his dislocated shoulder. He also wanted to help Dr. Franklin load up his plane.

Aran had mentioned to her that he thought that John might need surgery. After he had spent the night helping the road crew dig out Gerald's body and bring him back to town.

Lindsey slept on the way back, and Ruby couldn't blame her. Not really. She wished *she* could just sleep away the last couple of days.

They landed in Anchorage and it was only thirty minutes after that when Dr. Franklin landed his plane. An ambulance was waiting to take John to the hospital.

Aran barely looked at her.

She'd hurt him.

But he'd hurt her too.

They'd hurt each other.

It was only supposed to be a marriage of convenience—it wasn't supposed to form itself into anything else. But she had developed feelings for him. She had thought it was just attraction, but she admired him. She admired his strength, his tenacity, his tenderness.

She wanted so much more than just a fake marriage with him. They'd risked everything and for what? A Green Card? It seemed pointless.

She might want him to be more than just a convenient husband but she had ruined that now, and she knew that he didn't want to stay in the north. He didn't want to be really married to her, and she wasn't going to hold him back.

The right thing to do was to let him go. He had done her a huge favor, but that was all it was. All it could ever be.

This whole time she'd been trying to protect

her heart from getting hurt, and instead she'd set herself up for pain.

Her phone buzzed and it was Jessica. Agent Bolton was ready for their final interviews and was on his way to the hospital.

Ruby sighed.

Aran came over to her. "Did you get my mom's message?"

"Yes."

"Ready to get this over with?" he asked.

"Yes. I'm ready for this to end."

A strange expression crossed his face. "Right."

They rode back to the hospital in silence, and when they got there went straight up to the boardroom and sat next to each other, waiting for Agent Bolton to arrive.

"Ruby…"

"You don't have to say anything, Aran. For what it's worth, I'm sorry."

"I'm sorry too," he said gently.

The door opened and Agent Bolton stepped in. He smiled—and then frowned when he saw them. "Is everything okay, Doctors?"

"We lost a patient last night," Ruby muttered. "It was a bit difficult. He was a well-liked member of the Dutch Harbor community."

"It's affecting my wife particularly hard, Agent Bolton, because her father died in a similar circumstance when she was twelve." Aran glanced over at her. "That's why she's here, doing what she does. She doesn't want anyone to lose a loved one because there wasn't medical help when it was needed."

Ruby felt tears stinging her eyes as he spoke. She wiped them away.

"But even though I had everything there to save that man's life, I couldn't," she whispered. "Aran has been trying to teach me that there are some cases beyond our control, and that's sort of the curse of medicine. When it's beyond our control to save a life."

"I'm afraid the storm also triggered my post-traumatic stress disorder and brought back a lot of memories from the front."

Ruby knew Aran was saying these words to her, not Agent Bolton.

"So it's been a bit of a hard night for both of us."

"I can see that," Agent Bolton said gently. "And I can see that you two work very closely together. So I'm pleased to inform you, Dr. Cloutier that the United States Citizen and Immigration Services has granted you your Green Card."

Agent Bolton pulled out an envelope and slid it across the table to her.

"Congratulations, Dr. Cloutier. We're pleased to accept you as a citizen."

Ruby stared at the envelope in disbelief. She could go home. She could visit her mom and her brothers. She could visit her papa's grave. It was all she'd ever wanted…but somehow it wasn't everything.

It would mean the end of her marriage to Aran.

She looked over at Aran, who was staring at his hands, and wished that she had a little bit longer to get to know him. She wished she hadn't been so stubborn.

"Thank you," she whispered. "Thank you, Agent Bolton."

"You're welcome."

Agent Bolton stood up and left the boardroom. The silence in the room was so thick you could cut it with a knife. Ruby just stared at the envelope in disbelief.

"How long do we wait?" Aran asked.

"For what?" Ruby asked.

"You know for what," he said.

"A few months…no longer than that," she whispered.

Aran nodded. "I'm glad you got what you wanted."

"Thank you."

But even though she'd got what she wanted, her priorities had changed. She wanted Aran. She wanted what her parents had had.

Yesterday Gerald had died up on that roadside and, yes, it had crushed his family—but at least he'd *had* a family. He'd had someone to love him.

It had been the same with her parents. Her father's death had devastated Ruby's mother, but they'd had love. They'd shared love. They hadn't been lonely.

And this life that she had created, trying to protect her heart, had actually done more damage than good. She was alone and there would be no one to cry over her if she died. There was no one to share her life with.

She didn't want to live her life like that. She didn't want to live her life in fear any longer. She wanted Aran in her life and she wanted him as more than a convenient husband. She wanted him as a *real* husband.

"Aran..." She trailed off.

"A few months is good," he said quickly. "I want to return to San Diego."

"Oh," she whispered. "Right."

Her heart might have changed its mind about taking a chance on love, but she was a fool to think that Aran had. There had been no change of heart for him on that roadside. As far as he was concerned his job was done. She had her Green Card and that meant he was free.

"I think... I think I'm going to head for home." Ruby walked past him and didn't offer him a ride. She didn't think that he would come with her anyways. "I'm sure Sam is ready to get rid of Chinook."

Aran gave her a half-smile but wouldn't meet her eyes. "Right. I'll see you later?"

"Right."

Ruby left the board room as quickly as she could, clutching the Green Card. This was what she'd signed up for in the beginning. She'd always known there was a time limit to this marriage.

She just hadn't expected that she would fall in love with her fake husband.

She hadn't thought that she would fall in love at all.

Stop her!

That was what Aran's mind was screaming as he watched her leave the room, but he couldn't. He didn't want to be hurt by her rejection. That was why he didn't get involved in relationships. This was supposed to be just a simple marriage of convenience and it had been for so long, when they were apart, but now, after spending a short time with her, he was a lost man.

He'd known that the moment he'd seen her again. The moment she'd stood up to his mother, saying that she didn't want him on her team.

Ruby's words had hurt him at first, but after he'd calmed down he'd realized they were just words. He might have post-traumatic stress disorder from the IED explosion that had destroyed his career in the Army, but he wasn't the only one who was living with unresolved trauma.

Ruby had faced her demons last night when Gerald had died.

It hadn't just been about Gerald dying; she had been reliving what had happened to her father. She had given her whole life to stop others from dying like her father had—so much so that she'd never really dealt with the pain of losing him.

She'd avoided facing the reality of what had happened by trying not to let it happen again. But it wasn't lack of medical services that was the reason her father had died. It was the fact that his injuries hadn't been as simple as she'd thought as a child. They'd probably been just as catastrophic as Gerald's.

So he didn't hate her for lashing out at him. He hated himself for letting her into his heart, because now it was over. She had what she wanted. She didn't need him anymore.

Was that really accurate?

Aran had been so afraid of repeating what had happened to his parents. Maybe he'd really never accepted their divorce? The fact that his father hadn't been able to stay living in the north because his career was important, just as his mother's career was important to her.

His own career in the Army was over. He had accepted his discharge. So why was he so adamant about leaving Alaska and going back south? He had a couple of half-brothers and a half-sister there, but he could always visit them. What else did he have down there?

Nothing.

Here he had the chance of something more,

if he could just reach out and take it. He wanted to be with Ruby. He cared for her... he was falling in love with her. And it wasn't just lust—he'd gotten to know her.

If it didn't work out, then it didn't work out. But he would never know unless he actually tried. If she didn't love him, if she didn't want anything more from him, he would move on with his life—but he had to try. If he didn't he'd always wonder if he'd let go his one and only chance to be happy. His one chance to shake away the loneliness he felt.

Aran got up and ran after her as best he could with his leg aching.

"Ruby!"

Ruby turned around and he could see the tears in her eyes.

"Aran...?"

"Wait for me."

"What?" she asked.

He caught up with her and touched her face. "I love you."

Her dark eyes widened and welled with tears. "What?"

"I know. I know… But I've fallen in love with you. I know I told you that I couldn't make you any promises, and I still don't know…" He was rambling. He ran his hands through his hair. "I love you and I want to make this work."

"What about going back south? What about…?"

"I don't care."

"You told me it didn't work for your parents," she whispered. "How can it work for us?"

"Because I don't *have* anything in the south. My career is up here. I want to be here for you. I don't want to end this, Ruby. I want a chance to make things right."

Tears slid down her cheek. "I want to make this work too."

"You do?" he asked in disbelief.

"I love you as well. I was so afraid of falling in love because I was so afraid of what might happen to me if I lost the love of my life. I saw the way my mother mourned and I swore that I would never feel that way. But you made me realize that a life without love is not worth living. A marriage of convenience is not a marriage that I want to have. I want a *real* marriage. I want to love and I don't want to be alone anymore. I'm so tired of being alone. I didn't realize how alone I was until I met you."

She reached out and touched his cheek.

"I love you, Aran."

He pulled her into his arms and kissed her urgently. In that kiss he tried to convey all the emotions she'd brought out in him. How she had made him feel again. How she had brought him back to life. How she had *saved* his life.

"You've saved my life, Ruby Cloutier. You have saved *me*," he whispered.

She sobbed against his neck. "No. No, I didn't save you. *You* saved me."

They kissed again. Her arms moved around him and he never wanted to let her go. He was terrified about what the future held, but somehow the future that had looked so bleak when he had been discharged from the Army was looking brighter.

He hadn't realized how much of a fog he'd been living in until he'd seen her again. She had been the light waiting for him at the end of a very dark tunnel—just as he had been the light for her. They were guiding each other through the fog, showing each other the way home.

Jessica came down the hall. She was wringing her hands, but stopped when she saw them together.

"She got it?" Jessica asked.

Aran nodded and grinned down at Ruby. "She did."

Jessica let out a sigh of relief. "I'm so glad."

"And there's something else too, Mom," Aran said.

"What?" Jessica asked.

"We've decided to stay together and give this marriage a shot."

Jessica's eyes welled with tears and she smiled. "I'm so glad to hear that."

"Are you?" Aran asked.

Jessica nodded. "I messed up so bad with your father. I've always regretted that… And I've seen the way you two work together here and on the team. I'm so happy."

"Mom, it wasn't just you. It was Dad too." Aran stepped closer to his mother. "I'm sorry that I've blamed you all these years."

Jessica broke down in tears and he embraced her.

"I love you, Mom," Aran whispered. "I'm sorry for all the years that I didn't tell you that."

Tears slid down Jessica's face. "I love you too."

Ruby came forward and Jessica and Aran held onto her too.

Aran knew he had everything he could ever want in that moment. He'd been given a second chance. A way to make amends. And there was no way he was going to mess this up.

This time their marriage would be more than just a convenience. It would be a privilege.

His life started here—with Ruby.

EPILOGUE

One year later, north shore,
Great Slave Lake

RUBY GAZED UP into her husband's eyes as they stood on the north shore of Great Slave Lake. It was a bright sunny day, although there was a bit of a haze in the sky from some of the faraway forest fires that weren't uncommon for August in the Northwest Territories.

Aran was holding her hand as one of the elders from her village blessed their union. She was wearing a white gown, but it was a pretty simple gown, and it didn't hide the fact that there was a slight swell to her belly—she was five months pregnant.

Aran winked at her and she laughed softly.

Behind them sat the closest of their friends and family.

Her mother was crying softly and her brother sat next to her. Jessica sat next to Ruby's mother, and Aran's stepmother had flown up from San Diego. Lacey, Jack and their little girl Emily had flown down from Whitehead.

Mitchell had sent a card, as had Sam, who had promised to watch Chinook while Ruby and Aran enjoyed their honeymoon at a small fishing lodge up in Great Bear Lake for the next few days. Ruby was looking forward to relaxing there.

And beyond those few special guests who had come to witness their wedding vow renewal was a small table that held two precious photos. One of her papa and one of Aran's father.

It was everything she'd ever wanted. Because she'd never thought that when she'd married Aran six years ago she would one day be standing here, so close to home, pregnant and vowing to love him for real.

And she did love him.

She loved him with all her heart.

"And, in a renewal of your vows, do you, Aran, take Ruby to be your wife?"

"I do," Aran said, and slipped the ring he'd bought her on her finger.

"Ruby…"

The elder turned to her and spoke to her in her father's traditional language of Chipewyan. She'd had to relearn it because she'd never spoken it again after her father died, and relearning the language that had been lost to her had been like a rebirth.

It had righted a wrong.

"I do," Ruby answered, in both Chipewyan and English. She slipped the ring she had gotten for Aran on his finger.

"Then I am proud to announce the renewal of your vows, Aran and Ruby. May your lives be truly blessed."

Aran cupped her face and kissed her gently. Then he reached down and touched her belly. "My life is already blessed. I love you, Ruby."

"I love you too, Aran."

And she kissed him again. Surrounded by love, filled with love, and hoping for the brightest future possible. Even if that future was uncertain she was willing to face it— because she was no longer alone.

* * * * *